The Infiltrators

HOWARD REEDE-PELLING

Order this book online at www.trafford.com
or email orders@trafford.com

Most Trafford titles are also available at major online book retailers.

Printed in the United States of America.

ISBN: 978-1-4269-5227-2 (sc)
ISBN: 978-1-4269-5361-3 (e)

Library of Congress Control Number: 2010919498

Trafford rev. 05/03/2011

www.trafford.com

North America & international
toll-free: 1 888 232 4444 (USA & Canada)
phone: 250 383 6864 ♦ fax: 812 355 4082

TABLE OF CONTENTS

The Infiltrators

by

Howard Reede-Pelling

Two civic minded men, who are employed by a Customs Warehouse, discover a shipment of illegal firearms during their routine work and follow it through to prove their suspicions.

When they have stepped on some toes the authorities bail them out and then recruit the two to assist with their enquiries, they get involved too deeply and find their families at risk. After having been coerced by the police to trap the dealers, they in turn find that the gun running is just a 'front' for the real illicit trade; which is drugs run by a 'cartel'.

Then the conspiracy is further heightened by the cartels who enlist the aid of the two warehouse employees, to speed their 'goods' through the 'house'. Later, Ray and Gerry are enticed to act as 'double agents' for the cartel by infiltrating the opposition cartel.

This is the story of two very ordinary people who bite off more than they can chew, without help they could go down. Action packed and lively are the events herein depicted with many twists and an unenviable trail to the fairly predictable conclusion.

This is a MUST READ adventure tale.

Chapter One

As the light branch snapped, Ray overbalanced and fell through the tiles of the garage roof. His strong legs protruded between the runners which held the tiles in place. Ray supported himself by firmly grasping the runners and remained quite still, listening and watching for the lights of the nearby house, to illuminate. They did not, all became quiet again.

"You okay?" Gerry queried in a whisper from the bole of the tree above Ray.

"Yeah – hang on 'til I clear these loose tiles!" Ray cautiously did so, making very little noise.

"You climb down, I'll open the door." Ray ordered in a whisper. Ray lightly stepped onto the roof of the vehicle in the garage, dropped to the floor, and then unlocked the side door of the garage to admit his accomplice.

"Can't be anyone home." Gerry whispered.

"They would have to be woken by that racket!" Ray shook his head. "There's a car here, they may be heavy sleepers."

Both moved about with torches flashing cautiously, not wishing to reflect light through the one window, or the cracks of the doors.

"Here!" Ray exalted. "Let's get it open quietly!" The two eased screwdrivers under the nailed lid of the top wooden crate, which was one of three stacked in a corner. They had been covered by a tarpaulin.

"Yep." Ray whispered. "These are the ones they picked up today – the serial numbers tally – and I was right, illegal guns; very well packed!"

The garage light was switched on. The garage illuminated brightly.

"Not the slightest move or you both get it!" Joe Ratt snarled, thin moustache bristling above his tapered goatee. His beady eyes glistened as a slimy smile quirked his weedy features. Bert Luntz, his side-kick, quickly manoeuvred behind the two garage-breakers.

"They's clean." Bert declared. Joe waved the pistol he aimed at Gerry and Ray, motioning for the two to move away from the three crates of contraband.

"I'll put a hole in the first one to move!" Joe threatened, then to Bert. "Tie them up - good n' tight – separate!"

When both intruders were securely bound hand and foot, they were left sitting by the main garage door upon the concrete floor; Bert being given the pistol and ordered to guard the two men. Joe climbed into the vehicle and used the portable telephone always left within.

"Dermutt, its Joe, me an' Bert just caught two blokes that got in to the merchandise - ? No. I got 'em tied up. No, I dunno either of 'em but I think the heavy one works at the warehouse. I'm sure he's the one I got the delivery from!" There was a long pause as Joe listened to instructions; with an occasional; 'Yeah!' Of acknowledgement. Joe said.

"We'll find something there, don't want anything from here recognised, should be car parts or something at the tip there – okay?" Joe hung up the receiver in its cradle; then ordered.

"Help me lift 'em in the car; we're going on a little trip!"

The sleek black automobile purred along the highway. A seemingly endless queue of overhead lights slipped by monotonously, as the two bound captives struggled with their bonds, whilst laying most awkwardly on the back seat and floor of the vehicle; where they were unceremoniously dumped.

"That there is the wrecker's yard!" Joe told Bert, who was driving. "Use the lane at the other end – won't have to carry them so far!"

"Ugh – huh!" Bert agreed.

This little back road was rarely used and it was well pot-holed, due to the muddy nature of its structure. It was a most uncomfortable journey for the trussed pair who were attempting to undo each other's knotted bonds. Each jolt tore fingers away from the ropes of which they were attempting to rid themselves. The car turned a corner at the extreme end of the car-wrecker's yard.

"As I remember, the dam is over there behind those bushes where the gum trees are, we'll have to stop here and drag them through the fence." Bert allowed.

"Scout around for something heavy to hold them down!" Joe ordered. He peeked in to be sure their victims were still secure, then, satisfied, searched in a different direction to that taken by his underling; for a couple of heavy objects.

"Ain't nothin 'about. There's a log, but that might float." Bert worried, when their search brought the gun-runners together again.

"The bolt cutters are in the boot. Let's get through the fence and find an axle or an engine block. An engine block will hold them both down!" Joe ordered

He sent Bert to collect the bolt cutters. While Joe and Bert were searching, Ray had managed to extricate himself from beneath Gerry. Kneeling, he had lifted the button that kept the car door locked, with his strong teeth. He remained quite still when he observed Bert returning to the car, shushing Gerry to remain still also. When Bert went back to Joe, having acquired the bolt cutters, Ray opened the car door and both managed to roll out; still securely bound. Now able to move about better, Ray began to tug at the knots securing Gerry's hands. Their two kidnappers were struggling with an engine block from the wrecker's yard, and had managed to get it through an opening cut in the fence; when Gerry's hands were freed. Quickly he untied his feet, looked in to see that the keys were in the ignition switch, then took the driver's seat as Ray bundled himself back into the open rear door. The engine burst into life and amid a cloud of dust and a screeching of tortured tyres, the sleek black automobile careened away. Two very disgruntled no-goods were left stranded hurling the heavy engine block to the ground in disgust. By the time Joe had clawed the pistol from his pocket, their vehicle was well along the lane and hidden from view by the huge volume of dust, the speedy exit afforded. Two kilometres away from the wrecker's yard, Gerry stopped the vehicle and untied his immediate boss.

"Just a little hairy there for a bit." Ray grinned, as both settled in to the comfort of the front seats.

"Yes, I thought we had bought it." Gerry admitted.

"A bullet to the head and sunk in an abandoned dam as feed for the yabbies, does not appeal to me much!" Ray laughed. "Those two won't be very popular with this 'Dermutt'; whoever he is." Gerry also laughed.

"And to top it off, they have a long hike home – in the dark – hope the cops pick them up and pinch them for unlicensed pistols!"

The lucky escapees remained silent as they drove their hijacked automobile back.

"Can you recall the big bloke's name?" Ray asked.

"I remember him telling this Dermutt, 'it's Joe – I think – me and Mert' - !!!?"

"No – no, he said 'me and Bert', Bert with a 'B'. I remember very distinctly, he said 'Dermutt, its Joe – me and Bert just caught two blokes -!'" Gerry was adamant.

"Great." Ray applauded. "So the boss is Dermutt, the tall thin one with the moustache is Joe, and the sturdy one is Bert. Now, is this their car and was the address we went to theirs, or are they Dermutt's? Those two might just have been paid guards – then again – they could well live there. If this Dermutt has any brains he wouldn't stash contraband at his place!" Both fell silent again as they drove back to the suburbs; each racking his brains for answers to un-asked questions. When the familiar streets of the house of contraband came near, Ray stopped the vehicle outside a Police Station nearest to the house.

"They are not going to believe us, you know that don't you?" Gerry asked.

"Why not, it's the truth. My ropes are still in the car – their car – and it is probably registered at the address where the guns are stored. What more proof do they need?" Ray asked, very openly. The two entered the building and Ray asked the duty officer, if he could speak with a senior C.I.D. person. They were taken through a couple of doors and introduced to Detective Sergeant Ronald Shell.

"Be seated gentlemen. What can I do for you?" He cordially invited. Ray introduced himself and Gerry, and then elaborated upon the whole of the day's episode; including their 'breaking and entering.'

"You do realise that you will be charged for that." The detective warned.

"I am sure the magistrate will be lenient when this gun-running ring is proved and broken – besides – they intended to do away with us!" Ray frowned.

"Can you prove that?" "I was there, I was a witness." Gerry blurted.

"Even if we do arrest these men on the evidence of the contraband in their possession, they will not admit their intention to 'do away' with you; what proof do you have of that?" Detective Shell looked in query from one of his guests to the other.

"The tyre marks of the car, they are at the scene!" Ray suggested.

"And the rope they tied me with, it will match the other in the car." Gerry hopefully added.

"But did you not drive the car from there to here?" The detective insisted.

"Yes!"

"Well you could have just as easily driven it there as well, after you broke into the garage and stole it!" Detective Sergeant Ronald Shell sat smugly, clasping his hands in query.

"Let's go to the house and at least you will have the proof of the guns in the three crates!" Ray suggested.

Gerry drove the stolen automobile back to the house from which it originally came. Sergeant Shell's assistant, detective Frawly went in the car with him after the rope was recovered. Ray accompanied the senior policeman in the squad car after introductions were made. As the vehicles pulled up in the driveway, they noticed some lights were on in the house and the garage. The front porch light was switched on and a man appeared, dressed in pyjamas and a dressing gown. The slight, elderly man walked briskly over to the Detective Sergeant.

"Ah! You have found my stolen car – I haven't reported it missing yet!" He exclaimed, in apparent joy at his automobile's early recovery.

"And your name Sir?" Detective Shell asked.

"Johnson – Arnold Johnson – I thought I heard noises but thought it was possums, then after a while I decided to investigate. I have only just found that my car was stolen. They broke in through the roof you know!"

Sergeant Shell asked the owner.

"Do you mind if we see where they broke in?" He began walking to the garage.

"No – not at all – you can see the hole from here!" Arnold hurried along with the men. The detective sergeant looked about the garage, and then turned to Ray.

"Well! Where are these three crates you were talking about?"

"In the corner there, under that tarpaulin." Ray indicated the tarpaulin in question. The policeman lifted the article to reveal a small wooden table. Ray looked his astonishment; first at Gerry then to the detective sergeant.

"The rogues have done a switch!" Gerry expostulated. "We've been done!"

"So! I think you two had better return with us to the station!" Detective Frawly took both Ray and Gerry by their arms and bundled them into the police car.

"Can you manage your car now, Sir?" Detective Shell asked of the old man.

"Yes thank you Detective; you will charge them won't you?" He leered at the unfortunate Ray and Gerry as he made an obscene gesture of exaltation; not missed by the detectives.

"What now?" Ray asked.

"I will have to charge you with the breaking and entering, you have admitted to that." Detective Shell smiled over his shoulder at the uncomfortable pair in the back seat.

"And the car?" Ray asked, not expecting the answer that he got.

"Arnold Johnson is known to us. He is a convicted 'fence'; a dealer in stolen and smuggled goods. We believe your story and once we have it down and documented, we will travel to the wrecker's yard to verify that part of your story."

"But will we be charged for stealing the car?" Gerry asked earnestly.

"If you can prove you were at the wrecker's yard, then I ask myself. Why would you steal a car just to go to a wrecker's yard and then return the 'stolen' car to a police station?"

"Gosh, I hope that rope is still there." Ray fervently prayed.

"What are those names we wrote down at the station?" Detective Shell prompted.

"Dermutt, Joe and Bert!" Gerry obliged.

"Hmmmm! You are in a bit of trouble, aren't you?" The detective shook his head and frowned. "You may be safer in protective custody you know."

"Eh!" Ray lifted his eyebrows. "How so?"
We do know that Schloss has a couple of underlings who do his dirty work for him -!!"

"Schloss, who is Schloss? We don't know a Schloss do we Gerry?" Ray asked of his friend.

"No, I don't anyway." Detective Shell elaborated.

"Schloss is Dermutt – Dermutt Schloss. I was actually hoping that the contraband would be where you last saw it, but knowing

Schloss; I didn't really expect he would be that dumb. They secreted it away when you two went joyriding. We'll raid Johnson's pawnshop tomorrow but I will bet my boots that the goods won't be there either. Just a pity you never brought your suspicions to us first, instead of biting off more than you could chew!"

Having had a charge sheet made out for the petty breaking and entering, then a full statement duly typed and signed; the four set off to locate the wrecker's yard. It was three am. By that time and both Ray and Gerry were very tired. Gerry dozed off as Ray struggled to stay awake to guide the detectives. Torches gave enough light for the four to distinguish the automobile tracks. Detective Frawley set plaster casts of the tyre marks and all varieties of footprints, that were either side of the track and also those by the engine block left near the cut cyclone wire fence. A search by all eventually found the wire cutters, which were cast in the direction of the dam. The implement fell short by some twenty metres and it was carefully placed into a plastic bag, by the gloved Detective Frawly. The rope too, was placed into a plastic bag as further evidence.

"Time to go home!" Detective Shell announced. They began the return journey.

"Looks like your story tallies." Detective Shell stated. "No need to worry about the car theft. I'd rather let Mister Johnson believe that we are charging you though. What he doesn't know will help us all!"

"What was that talk about 'protective custody'?" Gerry queried.

"Good point!" Detective Shell nodded. "Joe Ratt and Bert Luntz are a couple of very desperate 'hit men'. We have not been able to pin anything onto them, because somebody higher than Dermutt Schloss, can pull some very heavy strings. I am extremely concerned that now you have opened this can of worms – somebody just may be tempted to go fishing!"

"They don't know who we are or where we live. Ray defended.

"Possibly!" Detective Shell mused. "But they do know where you both work and it would not surprise me, if that Dermutt Schloss has not already obtained all the information he needs about you two. He surfs the 'net' and he's good at it!"

Not much talk took place for the rest of the journey back to the police station. All were heavily engaged with their own thoughts. "Isn't it a bit premature to be thinking of protective custody?" Ray asked, eyelids drooping. "I mean, both Gerry and I are well equipped to defend ourselves!" He focussed his bleary eyes upon the detective.

"Muscles don't stop bullets very well and you should know how desperate those two are; by tonight's escapade. I should state very strongly that I believe you are both marked men. Ratt and Luntz are suspected killers, Schloss is a ruthless underworld organizer and whoever is his boss – we suspect a fellow named Slimmery – is the core of the contraband rackets in this state; if not the whole country!" He frowned at Ray. "If we don't provide some sort of protection for you, by tomorrow we may not need to. I hope you take this matter very seriously!"

Detective Frawley drove the squad car into the police parking area, behind the station. All alighted and entered the building. Two very agitated wives had reported husbands missing and word got to the police station. Both Ray and Gerry rang their wives to put the worried minds at ease. Detective Sergeant Shell obtained permission from his captain to post undercover officers at the homes of the two now at risk would-be sleuths. Ray and Gerry being so tired that they were allowed a few hours sleep in the officer's quarters. Detective Frawley began organizing full-time surveillance of both witnesses' homes and that of the 'fence', Arnold Johnson. The night's happenings were the beginnings of what the detectives believed, may be a break-through in a known gang of smugglers and gun runners. Detective Sergeant Ronald Shell was in earnest conversation with a Lieutenant Ferguson of the Special Branch; he was an under cover agent of the Secret Intelligence Organization.

"Slimy won't have the goods anywhere near his home, nor will they be at the pawnbroker's." Jason mused. "My guess is one of their warehouses – probably the one at Moorabbin – they wouldn't use the dockyards; too near to the import areas."

"We should strike immediately while Slimy feels comparatively safe." Ron suggested.

"It is now out of your hands, Ron. I'll get things moving!" Jason reached for the telephone and spoke authoritatively to his chief. "We have to move right now, Chief. I'll meet the squad at the Town Hall car park!" Jason replaced the telephone receiver upon its cradle.

"I shall come too!" Ron said.

"No. As I said, it is out of your hands now!" Jason was adamant.

"It's local authority that I carry – you may need me for any legal hitch." Ron persisted.

"Oh! Okay, just you and Frawley, but don't get in our way!"

Ray and Gerry were still sound asleep at the police station, as detectives Shell and Frawley accompanied Lieutenant Ferguson and his assistant, Graeme Carey. They contrasted oddly, did the two Secret Intelligence men. Lieutenant Ferguson towered over all from his two metres height. Mousy hair and small ginger moustache making him stand out (most un-common for under-cover men), and Graeme Carey being more slight than any of the other three in the un-marked car; made the two intelligence men a really odd-looking pair.

"The Chief will have organized papers for this operation by now, his close friend lives next door and he is a legal man capable of authorising all of our necessities. Sergeant Johnson, my squad leader, will have the papers with him – oh! Here's the town hall – they should be in the car park at the rear!" The Lieutenant confided.

The raid on Slimmery's Toy Factory was sudden, swift and very thorough; albeit fruitless. No sighting of illegal guns, drugs or any other form of contraband was detected.

"Damn the rotten luck. Not even a leaf of marijuana; how embarrassing!" Jason cursed.

"Where the hell have they stashed the stuff?" He thumped a huge right fist into his own left palm.

"They must have another storage that we don't know of yet." Graeme suggested.

"Yeah. Pack up lads – we're out of here!" Jason ordered.

All legal officers departed as swiftly as they arrived.

"What now?" Sergeant Shell asked of Lieutenant Ferguson.

"Surveillance, we will find their 'secret' cache and I will bet my badge that it is loaded!

Raymond Cress and Gerry Jones were awakened by a young constable.

"Coffee and toast gentlemen. It is seven fifteen a.m."

The two civilians were allowed refreshing showers after their breakfasts, and then were ushered into Detective Shell's office.

"Do you two feel up to going to work today?" He asked of them.

"Huh! I thought you said we were marked men!"

"Slimmery is too shrewd to do away with you immediately, he will bide his time. No doubt Slimy will have Schloss organize his two 'hit-men' to watch you for a bit, get to know your movements and week-end family activities. We think Schloss will be ordered to have someone, probably Ratt and Luntz, shadow you for a week; day and night at work and at home. Then when the heat is off – bingo! Another thing, they may have more contraband loaded and awaiting arrival. This could be on the water still. Even already in the warehouse where you work!" He eyed the labourers very carefully. "Agent Ferguson believes you can help us very well if you just go about your daily business as usual. We need a man or two 'inside' and you two are already there!"

"Aren't you sticking our necks out?" Ray frowned at Ronald Shell.

"Yes. But I feel that doesn't worry you two. You carried yourselves with quiet aplomb after escaping from an attempted murder and Lieutenant Ferguson will have his own 'protectors' planted at your place of employment; most likely they are already there! Could be a council worker, a gardener or even a telephone technician. You won't know and neither will Slimy, Schloss or their underlings. Will you help us? Needless to say, your 'breaking and entering' will be passed off as undercover work!" Detective Ronald Shell smiled encouragingly.

"Hey, I'm all for it!" Gerry eagerly expostulated.

Raymond Cress nodded as he grinned off-handedly.

"Why not?"

Chapter Two

"The fools bungled it Drew!" Dermutt growled as he thumped a very large fist onto the desk top, behind which a well-dressed business-man sat. Drew glared back from slitted deep-set tiny black orbs from which a glint of fire emanated. His look made Dermutt most uneasy, as the beefy little man attempted to explain his hirelings' failure to obey orders.

"The animals managed to untie themselves and got away - !!" Dermutt muttered.

"Incompetence! Bloody incompetence, I cannot use bunglers. Ratt and Luntz should have loaded them at the dam, and then looked for the weights; they would not have got away then!" Drew coolly blew a cigar-smoke ring in Dermutt's direction. "My Moorabbin Warehouse was raided and thoroughly searched. It may pay you to get the merchandise there, until Tuesday's pick-up; even if the place is being watched, the under covers won't expect I would use it again so soon. The stuff will be safe there now!"

Dermutt looked his surprise at the immaculately tailored man who made this unexpected statement.

"But, isn't it safer where we have it now? The Feds don't know where it is!"

"Too close to home. I have no desire to get the mongrels sniffing about my private properties."

Both men sat quietly as Drew pinched his chin between forefinger and thumb, then he crooned with his oily soft voice.

"I want the loaded goods to remain in the customs house. Do not attempt to take delivery just yet. Keep that pair of sticky-nosed snoopers under a very watchful eye and if they or the Feds get to find my goods; we will take them for ransom for the recovery. The loaded goods is pure stuff and worth many fortunes; the hardware is nothing by comparison. I am glad it was the hardware that they pounced upon and not the soft goods. See to it! Leave the clowns alone for now – dismissed!"

Dermutt Schloss left Drew Slimmery's office, shaking his head. 'He's too deep for me. I always feel insecure in there; he just bores right through a man.' Dermutt mused to himself.

"Damn those misfits of mine, they made me look bad to the boss!" He cursed out loud. A telephone call to Joe Ratt helped Dermutt to let off steam. He took his wrath out on his hireling, threatening blue murder if the two messed up again.

"Slimy wants us to lay low for a bit. Leave the soft stuff at the customs warehouse but we have to move the artillery. It's going to – er – no. I will call over just to be sure you get it right this time; expect me in fifteen minutes!"

Dermutt hung up, leaving Joe in a quandary.

"Sir, you had better listen to this!" An officer suggested to Sergent Lysle Johnson.

"Roll it!" Lysle ordered. He heard the taped conversation between Dermutt Schloss and Joe Ratt with keen interest.

"Sounds as if Schloss is still putting his mouth on the blower." Sergent Johnson grinned. "Give me a copy of that, I'll take it to the boss straight away!" He ordered. Lieutenant Ferguson listened very intently to the tape that Lysle set into the tape recorder upon his boss's desk. "That ties Schloss and Slimy together and also implicates Joe Ratt.

Are you sure the trace was the right connection?" He asked, offhandedly, knowing full well how thoroughly his team worked. "No doubt about it Jason. Is it time to do the customs shed over?" Jason shook his head. "No! Slimy wants no movements yet awhile. It will be safe left there for a day or two. Get word to Ray Cress and have him discreetly look about the place. See if he can locate the 'sleeping' shipment. Be sure he knows not to disturb it, I only wish to locate it for the present!"

"Yes Sir!"

Ray and Gerry went about their duties as normal, each carefully crossing off their checklists those commodities on the lists which were regular orders and known innocent goods. The customs warehouse which was their domain was huge, and the crates of goods stacked so high as to reach the roof at times.

"Talk about a needle in a haystack!" Gerry complained.

"Stick at it, we'll get there!" Ray encouraged. "We don't have much to cover. Remember that we know the destination code and Slimy's usual ports of departure; that cuts the search down to about five percent."

"Five percent of billions is still a powerful search." Gerry griped.

"Don't exaggerate." Ray chided, then exclaimed in earnest. "Hey. I think I have something here – double check it Gerry!" Gerry did so.

"Yes!" The other big man agreed.

"Shh! Act natural, we don't know who may be watching. Continue tallying as normal." Ray and his assistant continued their checking, having noted the bay, row and tier number of the valuable crate of contraband. Lunch time found Gerry in the dining room of the warehouse complex, a position from which he could easily keep an eye upon the warehouse stock, through the wall-long observation window. Ray had cause to hurry along to the shop on the opposite side of the wharf road. It was a general store that catered very profitably to the waterside clientele. Once Ray had made his purchase, he casually sauntered over to the public telephone which was situated in a quiet corner of the store.

"Lynton – intelligence!" Came clearly through the receiver.

"Cress! Get a message to Lysle or Jason, that the package is located and I await directions!"

"That it?"

"Yes!" Ray replaced the receiver and returned to the warehouse.

Meanwhile, inside a plain panel van with darkened windows, two S.I.O. agents were listening-in to a conversation between Dermutt Schloss and Joe Ratt.

"Slimy reckons that the goods will be safer at the Moorabbin joint, now that the Feds have raided it; he thinks the heat's off there. I reckon its best left where it is, but, he's the boss and we gotta carry out orders. Take one of the works wagons and make it look like a legitimate order being serviced. Do it during business hours and wear the company's bloody uniform. It has to be done now – before lunch – pick up Bert and act like real employees; don't rush!"

Dermutt left his underling's home and casting a casual glance at the van inconspicuously parked in the shade of a tree, went upon his way; hoping that his assistants did not bungle this mission. A very ordinary-looking sedan with a male and a female agent posing as a married couple followed the glossy limousine that Joe and Bert drove in, to the Moorabbin warehouse of Drew Slimmery. The officers noted the miscreant pair enter the premises and a little later, exit them, wearing the company's uniforms. Joe and Bert climbed into one of the company panel vans and went to collect the contraband crate of guns. The officers kept in comfortable sight of the van, hoping that the gun-runners were not aware that they were being followed. They were not!

"Riley and Dean – condition green – at Stewart's Storage. Send a wagon for two. Over and out!"

The message came jubilantly to Jim Lynton at the switchboard. He relayed the message to the officers standing by. As Joe and Bert were manhandling the crate of contraband out of storage, the two S.I.O. officers pounced. When the villains were safely handcuffed, the back-up team arrived. Photographs were taken of the scene and especially the crate and its serial numbers including the address of destination. The video rolled as the crate was opened and its contents displayed. Joe and Bert were taken into custody, both claiming that they were just employees doing a pick-up and delivery. Late that afternoon, Drew Slimmery's lawyer had both men bailed out of the lock-up on a technicality. The fact that they were just employees doing as directed was the winning factor. To their knowledge it was a legitimate crate of goods to be moved from here to there; nothing more. Smugly, the 'hit-men' cockily strode from detention to freedom. Their demeanour was far from cocky when they were being lambasted verbally by Dermutt Schloss; later that evening.

"You flaming idiotic pair of dolts! Can't you do anything right?" Dermutt fumed.

"Slimy is ropable, he wants your flippin' heads!" Dermutt strode quickly to and fro across his office carpet.

"Do you two know how much your bungling has cost us? Not to mention the fact that the operation is now blown wide open. Our 'fence' is under suspicion, the Feds know our Moorabbin joint is one of the holding areas and the boss's privacy has been breeched. Financially, the boss has lost one cargo worth many thousands plus your bloody legal fees and they may even impound the rotten truck. No wonder Slimy wants you two replaced; permanently!" He glared belligerently at his two crestfallen accomplices.

"But Boss -- !!" Joe began.

"Shut up, I'm thinking!" Dermutt ordered.

Dermutt sat at his office table, drumming his fingers thoughtfully for a full two minutes, and then calmly addressed his aides.

"You two had better take time off. Go fishing or bowling. The under covers are watching you like hawks. They know you'll bungle about and lead them somewhere that we don't want them to know about. Here –" Dermutt opened his safe and tossed two wads of notes towards his henchmen.

"Go interstate until your case comes up, maybe that'll take a bit of the heat off proceedings down here; they should follow you. Leave immediately and contact me through 'Burnsie', in a couple of weeks – go!" Both miscreants nodded, said 'thanks Boss' and departed. Dermutt reached for his telephone.

"Hi, Charlie? Got a job for you and Bernie!"

Overnight, the 'soft goods' that Ray and Gerry located for the S.I.O., was quickly replaced by plastic containers of flour and left as if it were the contraband. Lieutenant Ferguson had his men complete the operation swiftly in the small hours of the night. Ray being seconded to distract the usual overnight caretaker for expediency and so to take less risk of Drew Slimmery finding out about it. The exchange was accomplished within ten minutes and when Ray witnessed the short flashing of the blue police warning lights as the S.I.O. departed, he returned with the overnight caretaker to the main storage area; just to 'double-check' before leaving the man to his duties.

"You look tired dear." Cindy noted, as her husband snuggled into bed beside the curvaceous, honey-haired centre-fold model. "You are working too many long hours. We are comfortable enough; you don't need to drain yourself dear. Why do you do it?"

Her beautiful blue eyes lusted after her man as she placed sweet lips tenderly upon the tired man's cheek – nose – forehead – neck, then lovingly upon the tightly closed lips of the man she loved. He responded by embracing his wife lightly as he returned her kiss fondly.

"Can't tell you just yet Sweet and I am too tired for that. Could we leave it until tomorrow when I will be fresh and vibrant?" He squeezed Cindy again, then after another taste of her lips, rolled over and immediately fell asleep.

"Yes Dear, I suppose!" Cindy whispered to herself as she sighed.

"Tomorrow, it is always tomorrow."

Cindy called to Ray.

"Are you ready dear? Have them while they are fresh; I'll pour the coffee!"

"Right-oh, timed it nicely!"

Ray gave Cindy a light kiss upon the cheek as he sat and took a thankful sip of the beverage prepared for him. Cindy sat near her man and partook of her own morning wake-me-up.

"You were wonderful this morning Dear, I enjoyed your company so much; thank you." Her bright eyes twinkled happily. Ray leaned over and kissed her upon the mouth.

"Gosh!" Cindy exclaimed. "A bacon flavoured kiss!"

"Oops, sorry Sweetheart – must run – work to do. See you tonight!"

Ray pecked his wife again, and then hurriedly departed. As he left the house, he caught sight of the man reading a newspaper as he lazed in the morning sunshine upon a seat in the park opposite Ray's home. 'Good, they are still on the job.' He thought to himself, and then mused.

''I don't think it's really necessary though!"

Gerry Jones was awaiting Raymond Cress at the office entrance to their warehouse employment.

"There was a message from Sergeant Johnson. I think he's the squad leader; he reckons Lysle needs us urgently!"

"What. Did he ring here?" Ray asked, incredulously.

"Yeah! Monty called me in soon as I clocked on!"

"What does Lysle want?"

"Damned if I know. Only that it's quite urgent and that a car will get us from the east corner. Quick, we have to hike along. It should be waiting now, he said in five minutes and that was ten minutes ago!"

Ray quickly clocked on, and then the two big men hurried to the arranged appointment. An unknown man in an un-marked car was keenly waving the pair to make haste. He flashed an official I.D. at them as Gerry and Ray piled into the back of the vehicle.

"What's the great rush?" Ray asked of the driver.

"Can't tell you Sir, sorry. Lieutenant Ferguson will enlighten you; I don't usually work alone but we are understaffed and this is most urgent!"

"How far do we have to travel?" Gerry inquired.

"Five minutes – city office." The driver answered, and then became quiet. They motored on until the sedan swung into a small lane, then turned into a car parking area behind a big city office block. Their driver hurried the two workmen into the building and then up three flights of dimly lighted stairs. The trio entered an office where a secretary nodded to the driver before he knocked, then went through a door marked 'Lieutenant Jason Ferguson'. The Lieutenant arose to greet his guests. There were two other men and a lady already in the office. All were invited to be seated; they did so, and then waited patiently as Jason frowned. He picked up a sheaf of papers and browsed through them quietly before looking up at Ray and Gerry.

"My contacts have notified me that Joe Ratt and Bert Luntz have been sent interstate, to put us off the scent."

"But that's no reason to drag us in here -- !!" Ray began.

Jason held up a hand for attention.

"Just listen!" Ray nodded and awaited the tall man's explanation.

"Schloss made a 'phone call to Charlie Quin and Bernie Lloyd. Both are known kidnappers." The Lieutenant gazed steadily at Gerry and Ray, and then expanded.

"I have doubled the cover on your homes for a while; we suspect that Slimmery may be thinking of getting to you two through your wives and kids!"

"What?" Both Gerry and Ray arose; surprise upon their faces.

"Don't be overly worried." Jason calmed. "Your families are in no danger. Gerry, we have supplied an agent as 'nanny' for Jo-Anne, she will be stationed by the school during school times and live-in at other times; in association with Wilbur. I have a twenty four hour watch at both your homes. I feel by the week's end we will have trapped Schloss and his men. Slimmery could be different though, he covers his dealings too well. My sources agree that Slimmery will need a 'ransom' to make certain his valuable delivery goes through. We are ready and waiting. The next move is up to Slimy or his crony, Schloss!"

A short stocky man with an air of quiet authority spoke.

"Mister Cress – Mister Jones. We appreciate that you are making sacrifices and your assistance in this matter, is of national importance to your country."

Ray and Gerry frowned at the man.

"To whom am I speaking?" Ray inquired.

"Oh, sorry!" Jason Ferguson intervened. "Ray and Gerry. This is Chief Flemming, Captain Vaughn and Lieutenant Amy Truscott; Chief Flemming's secretary!"

The two civilians nodded their recognition as all shook hands. Chief Flemming continued.

"The S.I.O. has been aware of Slimmery's operations for many months but could not pin-point his shipments. We have had all of the waterside warehouses under surveillance, but without success - until you two stumbled into our infrastructure. The illegal firearms are a diversion from the true and valuable contraband. Illicit drugs, world-wide!"

Both Gerry and Ray looked their amazement at the enormity of the un-folding events. That the pair were unsuspectedly thrust into international implications of drugs and gun-running which was now threatening, not only their once placid life-style but also the very safe-keeping of their immediate families; began to dawn as an out-of-control phenomenon in which the two were beginning to regret becoming involved. Both now realised that their little foray into police work, had back-fired and they had indeed, bitten off more than they could chew!

"Chief Flemming." Ray cautiously inquired. "Presuming our families are safe under surveillance, how are we so important to you. I thought our work at the warehouse was sufficient; over and done with?" Chief Flemming smiled wryly as he shook his head.

"I suppose you do have the right to understand!"

Chief Flemming 'harrumffed' as he cleared his throat before elaborating.

"There is a huge international cartel of drug-runners under world-wide scrutiny. I and my colleagues are in charge of this country's implication and all states are as one in an effort to at least stamp out this one cartel. We are just at the tip of the iceberg momentarily, even though most of the state's leaders, dealers, carriers, importers and associated riff-raff, are known; hitting the top people involved has been very difficult to legally prove. Until now, we had no idea that the gun running was a cover for the drug shipments. We knew the drugs were coming in and we knew also that the guns were coming in, but we had no proof that the two operations were linked – until now!"

The Chief pouted heavily at the two civilians.

"Your interference has finally linked Slimmery to both activities. This is a break-through for us, and we need you as outsiders to consolidate the foundations of this link; so as to trap the bosses of both operations. A sound connection between the two will make convictions so much more legally binding!"

Ray sat wide-eyed as he let this information sink in; then asked.

"What do you have in mind for us?"

"Sooner or later, and we expect sooner, you or Mister Jones may be approached to be coerced into co-operating with the cartel; with your families welfare threatened if you don't co-operate. We have all the protection we feel is necessary in place, but that will not stop threats. These are desperate people with money as their God. An odd murder here and there is nothing to them. We would prefer to have our own experienced people 'inside', but much of our network is known on the internet. You are two fresh faces who are not in any way connected to law enforcement bodies. As 'sleepers', you could easily be sucked into their network; especially so as you have shown courage under fire and the fact that Schloss and Slimmery need to replace those bunglers, Ratt and Luntz!"

The other officer, Captain Vaughn, interposed. "We are asking you two to allow yourselves, as inconspicuously as you can, to be drawn into service for the cartel. You will be sworn in as legal assisting officers for so long as you are useful to us. You will have the full protection of the law and we feel that you will only be used by the cartel, in your present capacity – organizing the slick delivery of the contraband!"

Captain Vaughn indicated the female officer.

"Lieutenant Truscott here is Chief Flemming's secretary and has full control of all matters relating to your families. Your families will have access to her at the top and immediate response in any emergency which may arise. Sorry to rush you into this but time is of the essence!" Chief Flemming gazed deeply at the two civilians.

"Your country needs you!" He urged. Gerry and Ray exchanged glances.

Both nodded agreement.

CHAPTER THREE

"Flemming says today!" A man raking leaves said to Ray, as he continued working. Ray, not really surprised, grunted.

"Ugh – huh!" But did not look at the man, as he had already seen the workman whilst un-locking his garage door. Ray set his vehicle into forwards gear and motored to work. At the warehouse car park the big foreman was accosted by a short stocky grey-haired man in his mid-forties. He was well dressed and appeared to be a business-man. He carried a small brief-case.

"Would you be Raymond Cress, the foreman in charge of shipments?" The man asked, oilily.

"Yes Sir that is me. What can I do for you?" Ray acknowledged and asked.

"Business proposition. I am Gunther Berrimann – importer, here is my card."

He offered a business card to Ray, who accepted it.

"Shouldn't you be addressing the office staff?" Ray asked, with a smile.

"Very astute!" Gunther applauded, then chummily confided. "The truth is, the office staff has to stick to guide lines and regulations. I have lots of urgent shipments which need to be given a higher priority. My stock needs to be serviced immediately it arrives and it would aid my business immeasurably, if perchance the goods could be hurried through customs a little more quickly than usual. My connections will offer a rather large stipend for a person of some authority within the warehouse, who could arrange this action with some expediency. Such a man as yourself will benefit very well financially – does the position interest you at all?"

Gunther Berrimann withdrew a very large wad of banknotes from his inside coat pocket. He ruffled through the sum of money as a card-sharp would, to impress. Ray pouted, as he allowed himself to greedily eye the small fortune.

"Is that a down payment?" He asked.

"Yes, but not here, privately at lunch. Do you know 'The River Café', further down the wharf road?" Ray nodded.

"Just keep this little chat to ourselves until we have properly discussed arrangements. Can you be there at say – er, what time would suit you best?" Gunther cocked an eyebrow.

"Twelve-thirty. I have three-quarters of an hour then!"

"Fine, you will keep this confidential?" Gunther queried. Ray nodded, and then strode off, leaving the stocky man behind. Ray noted a slick limousine departing the car park as he entered the office of the warehouse complex. A new security guard accosted Ray as he went into the changing room to don his white jacket. The guard flashed an S.I.O. badge.

"Time to wire you Sir!" Ray allowed the agent to install a listening device to his person. "All set. Good luck Mister Cress!" The officer cheerily offered. "Thanks!" Both men went about their duties.

At the appointed time, Ray approached an isolated table towards a very quiet corner of 'The River Café'. Gunther Berrimann was already seated and awaiting him. The man scowled as he saw that Ray was accompanied by another person.

"I understood that we were to talk alone!" Gunther opened the conversation.

"Relax!" Ray grinned. "This is Gerry. He is my second-in-command. I have him do the dirty work. We always work together and he has a young family to support. Gerry is right with us. We will be stronger that way; trust me!"

Ray exuded confidence as he introduced Gunther to his partner.

"Yeah. I know!" The businessman unexpectedly acknowledged.

"You know?" Ray queried himself surprised.

"I am a businessman; I need to check out my employees. I also know that you foiled one of my shipments. That surprises you, doesn't it? I need to know with whom I am dealing." A waitress appeared.

"Your orders?" She asked.

When all had received coffee and sandwiches, they got down to the finer details of the work expected of the storemen. Gunther then finished off the dealings with –

"I shall notify just you, Ray, when a shipment is in and needs to be serviced immediately. Here is the down payment. I will add another fifty percent seeing as you have a partner. Share it!" He arose and made to go. Ray confirmed.

"If there are any problems, can I contact you on your business card number?"

Gunther Berrimann nodded, and then left. Ray discreetly placed the large wad of notes into an envelope which he had brought along for the purpose. Ray spoke into his collar.

"Hope you got that, he's gone!"

In the office changing room the security guard took the bribe money from Ray, to be checked by the forensic department.

"Gee!" Gerry begrudged. "I could have done so much with my half of that lot. Looks like crime really does pay!"

"Only until you get caught spending it." Ray cryptically grinned. "I rest better with honestly earned money!"

"Yeah!" Gerry admitted. "Well, come on you slacker. Gunther needs his latest shipment of flour – er – merchandise, to be quickly processed."

It was urgently pushed through with no hold-ups what-so-ever. A delivery van arrived for the shipment shortly before two-thirty. Ray had Gerry organize the loading and receipt signing. Both men were well aware that the supposed 'high quality' drug shipment, would be traced to it's destination both physically and electronically, by the hidden 'bug' supplied by the S.I.O.; when they exchanged the contraband for harmless flour.

"Someone has taken you for a fool Dermutt! That was our most valuable shipment ever – pure stuff – and we didn't even get the lid off. The 'Feds' were all over the place as soon as it was signed in. Now I have lost my 'cutting' centre at Richmond. You are a bungling fool!"

Drew Slimmery was in a raging temper. He thumped his desk-top, and then aimed a pistol at his unhappy second-in-command.

"A man ought to blow you away. You are as big a bungler as Ratt and Luntz!"

His beady eyes blazed angrily at the cowering Schloss.

"But, I thought the place at Richmond would be safe. I don't know how the Feds got on to it!"

Thoughts that his two 'new hands' may have been responsible came flashing through, but he shook his head; dismissing that idea. They were too new to have any idea of the contents; they may have suspected guns; but never dope."

Drew noted the slight shaking of Dermutt's head.

"What – what? It's something I should know. Tell me, or I swear, you cop one!" Dermutt raised his hands palms towards his boss.

"It's just those two snoopers. I hired them as you suggested and they went for it, but they are only employees; the money lure went big with them. They don't know about the dope, they think I deal in guns. I am sure they're clean. Just big muscle-bound oafs. No, I reckon the S.I.O. has one of our lines bugged. They were onto us too quick!"

Drew Slimmery replaced his pistol into the holster behind his back. He mused thoughtfully to himself. 'Yes, yes, of course. But I think it is you and Johnson who are bugged. No one can use my line; I have a good man at the exchange that caters for my needs there.' Drew calmed quickly.

"Get rid of Johnson – he knows too much. Change your office overnight, move into the city, use an established line. Personally bring the details to me and don't trust those two new men until they have proved themselves. Have them take out Johnson!"

Dermutt stood, mouth agape; then queried.

"But Boss, they aren't 'hit men'; they are of more use to push the shipments. I don't think --?"

"That's right. You don't think! Do as you're told. If you are sure of your new men, let them prove themselves, they are to take out Johnson. See to it!"

Dermutt left Drew Slimmery's office still shaking his head. 'It won't work, they are not the type. I reckon losing a shipment has tipped the boss's mind.' The stocky man sat in his car, thinking deeply after his unhappy meeting with Drew. It was fifteen minutes before he devised a plan of action. Determined, Dermutt motored to the vicinity of the exit from the waterfront car park. He awaited Raymond Cress. When the foreman drove out to go home, after his work day was over; Dermutt Schloss discreetly followed.

Ray stopped at a Milk Bar to pick up some supplies to take home. When he arrived back at his car with arms full of purchases, Dermutt Schloss was awaiting him. In mild surprise, Ray addressed the man.

"Hello Mister Berrimann, fancy meeting you here. Do you live out this way?"

He asked, cordially. Dermutt nodded whimsically as Ray placed his purchases into the boot of his car.

"Need to talk to you. Hop in my car will you?" Both settled comfortably.

Ray looked quizzically at the stocky businessman.

"We have a problem!" Dermutt gravely said. "That last shipment went astray; the Feds took it and closed down one of my business houses."

Ray feigned surprise.

"Gosh Mister Berrimann, that's a rum deal. How do I fit in to this?"

Dermutt peered closely into Ray's eyes.

"That is what my boss wants to know. He reckons that as you and your mate are new and unproven, that you may be the cause of our problems!"

"But our job was just to move your wares quickly and efficiently through the 'house'." Ray frowned.

"Yes! I know that and so does my boss, but, he wants you two to prove your loyalty to our cause."

"How?" Ray questioned.

"We believe out 'phones are bugged or perhaps our 'fence' has leaked information to the S.I.O. The boss has ordered that you two 'take care' of him. His name is Johnson and he is the bloke at the house where you broke in and found our merchandise!"

Ray Cress was shocked at the unexpected proposal. That he and Gerry should 'take care' of an old man. Ray had no doubt about what was intended for them to do; but murder? He worried.

"You mean we have to --!?"

"Yes. You have to. There are millions of dollars involved here and we can't have any loose ends. You will get a 'fee' for it over and above your usual, but it has to be neat and clean – no traces back here – then once proven; both of you are in for a share of the goodies." The smooth businessman oilily ogled at his newest accomplice. "You two can be relied upon, I hope, otherwise things may get a bit sticky!"

"Yeah! It's a bit more than we expected, but if the cash is there, leave it to me. Gerry and I can handle it - when?"

Ray gave out an air of quiet confidence, but was seething inside at the position he had been wiggled into by this domineering stranger.

"Tonight; the boss wants it now!"

Ray grunted, and then returned to his own vehicle. Dermutt Schloss motored away, a satisfied smirk upon his face.

"Strewth. That was easy!" He muttered to himself. "If these two can deliver who needs Ratt and Luntz – they can rot interstate"

He began his search for an office somewhere in the city proper, to accommodate the other half of his orders. Ray drove home very thoughtfully, knowing that he could be watched, not only by the agents of the S.I.O. but also quite possibly by Dermutt Schloss's men and also Berriman may have a watch on him. At this time, Ray was unaware that Schloss and Berrimann was one and the same person. He had never met or even seen Schloss; only had word of him. Once home, Ray placed his purchases upon the kitchen table. Cindy called from the laundry.

"Hello Dear, did you have a good day?"

The vivacious young lady rushed to greet her lover.

"I am so glad that you came home early. I hope you haven't forgotten our date this evening!"

"Oh!" Ray turned in surprise. "Is that this evening? No, I didn't forget, I mean - I - yes! Sorry Sweet, I did forget - gosh - I am in a pickle!"

He turned very worried eyes towards his beautiful wife.

"Is there any chance at all I can wriggle out of it Sweet? I have something of national importance to attend tonight!" Cindy looked her astonishment.

"National importance?" She asked, with the faintest of a quirk about her dainty mouth. Ray looked deeply and seriously into her eyes, and then gently kissed his wife. He gave her a loving cuddle.

"Yes Sweet, I have been ordered to kill a man!"

Cindy suddenly pulled away, the better to study her husband's face.

"You are serious!" She stated.

"I'm afraid so. I'm not going to of course, but I have been ordered to do so."

Cindy sat down, ashen faced.

"What have you gotten into? I mean you are just a foreman in a warehouse. You never really explained why those men keep watching and Natalie is frightened to say much on the telephone. Now you have me very worried. Don't just shake your head with a silly grin; it doesn't help!" Cindy implored. "Please tell me dear, what is going on – please!"

Ray moved over and gave his loved one a comforting cuddle, he tenderly whispered into her ear between gentle kisses.

"Now don't you go making an emu out of a chicken. There is no real need for panic. Don't get all fussed up about those undercover people, they are just making sure that I can't be got at through you; the same goes for Natalie and the girls. I uncovered a gun-running gang through the warehouse and the Federal Police need me to locate other shipments; that's all. There is no real danger. We are well protected."

Cindy peered earnestly into her man's eyes.

"But – but you just said that you have to kill a man. What did you mean?"

Ray eased his wife into a chair, and then sat down himself. Quietly he whispered.

"I am not supposed to tell you too much Sweetie, the less you know the safer you are. The house may be full of 'bugs', listening devices. The police are not listening, however we don't know if anyone else has broken in and planted something whilst we have been out. So the less we say, the better; other than our daily routine matters! I have been approached by a man who recruited me into the gang of gun-runners as the police wanted. To prove my loyalty, they need for me to kill a man. I will find ways around it – you know I couldn't do anything like that – trust me Sweet and everything will be fine. Don't ask any more awkward questions, I'll tell you when it's all over. Shouldn't be more than a week or so!"

The night had barely settled in as Ray called upon his friend and workmate, Gerry. Natalie received him warmly.

"What a pleasant surprise!" She exclaimed. "Please come on in, Gerry is putting the children down; coffee?"

"No thanks Natalie. The truth is, some overtime has cropped up and it is extremely urgent. Hope you don't mind."

"G'day Ray! Don't mind what?" Gerry boomed from the corridor.

"Boss has some overtime!" Ray stated, with a wink only seen by Gerry.

"Oh!" Gerry said. "Urgent is it? Better scoot then. Do you mind terribly Love?" Gerry kissed his wife as he grabbed his coat.

"If the work is important, I suppose you must go. Drive safely Darling!"

After driving around some back streets the while he watched the rear-view mirror, Ray eventually stopped the vehicle by a public telephone. He had an urgent conversation with Lieutenant Jason Ferguson, and then resumed his journey.

"All set?" Gerry asked. Ray nodded.

"Yes. Hope the old man doesn't try something foolish!"

"Do you think he will? He seems active enough." Gerry grinned, and then added. "I always wondered what it would be like to 'bump' somebody off."

"Ha!" Ray laughed. "Blowed if I don't think you would enjoy it. You certainly look the type." Gerry smiled at his friend's mild raillery.

"Could you imagine young Jo-Anne at school, bragging about her daddy; the 'hit man'."

"Heaven forbid!" Ray shook his head, seriously. "It is getting like that in some of the other Western countries. Even school kids carry death-dealing weapons over there; we are just amateurs!"

The foreman had a morbid tone to his voice. They drove in silence for a quarter of an hour; then Gerry called.

"Here we are, let's go in and 'do away' with this old man."

Arnold Johnson peered through the clear glass side windows of his front door.

"Yes, who is it?" He querulously asked.

"Dermutt had us call 'round; we have arrangements to make with you!" Ray quietly told the man.

"Dermutt! Why ain't Joe an' Bert doin' it?"

"They've been sent on a job interstate." Ray confidently advised.

The door opened a little, tentatively.

"I don't know you, Dermutt should have -!!"

Gerry pushed the door open suddenly. Arnold was thrown backwards and staggered to regain his balance. Ray hurried forwards, grabbed the old man by both arms and held him against the wall. Arnold struggled violently to escape but was no match for the stronger, virile young giant.

"Search for weapons!" Ray ordered.

Gerry did so. He took a pistol from the man's right hand and another from his hip pocket.

"Expecting trouble?" Ray sarcastically asked.

"Hey. I know you. You are the clowns that busted into my garage and nicked my limo', aincha. Have ya come to bash me?"

"No." Ray quietly said, as he yanked one of the hallway curtains down and had Gerry bind the man's arms.

"Make sure he can't wriggle out!" Gerry did so.

"What's doin'?" Arnold asked, as the three motored along the freeway.

"Berrimann reckons you tipped off the Feds, so we got to get rid of you." Ray grimly advised.

"But I didn't; I ain't done nothin'!" Fear showed in the old man's eyes. "Who – who's Berrimann. I don't even know a Berrimann. I didn't do nothin', honest!"

"Shut up!" Gerry glared at the old man, and then asked of Ray.

"Does Berrimann work for Schloss, or is it the other way round?"

Ray shook his head.

"Wouldn't have a clue, they may not know each other"

"But Berrimann ordered this old codger out of the way and he said his 'shipment' was bungled. Yet the guns at Arnold's house belonged to Schloss. They must know each other!" Gerry worried.

"Heh, heh!" Arnold laughed. "Yez've been took. Schloss often uses other names. He's prob'ly this Berrimann codger. If'n he is, he knows I'm on his side. He knows I don't squeal. Why do he want me out of the way?" Arnold puzzled. Ray answered.

"Not your problem, Arnold!"

A flashing blue light at the radiator of a car parked amongst the shrubbery of the freeway, caused Ray to pull over. A plain clothes S.I.O. agent flashed his badge.

"Jason sent us." He stated.

Gerry hustled Arnold out of their vehicle and handed him to the two officers. They took the old man away. Gerry and Ray returned to their own homes.

Chapter Four

Arnold Johnson was informed of his predicament by Jason Ferguson, when he was secreted into the Lieutenant's office.

"It is only a matter of time before you blokes have your so-called, 'mates', dob you in for something; deserved or not. For your own safety we are obliged to give you a new identity. You will be moved interstate, out of sight out of mind. Stay here and the 'mob' will get you and finish the job!"

Jason looked deeply into the ruffled old man's troubled eyes.

"Wot about me house and me business? A man can't just up and leave it."

Lieutenant Ferguson spoke with authority.

"We are giving you a chance to live on. A draft is being drawn up for you to give an agent of ours, 'power of attorney' over your affairs. All of your holdings will be sold up in your name. Arnold Johnson will be announced dead. A body collected from a bush dump. For your own safety, you have to appear to have been 'done away with'! Co-operate with us and much of your illegal operations' will be overlooked. Are you with us on this?" Arnold looked a little relieved.

"Sure, sure. I always wanted a way out. A man's gettin' too old for this caper anyway!"

"You did a good job making it look like a tree fell and squashed him. My boss was impressed. Now, I have two shipments coming in. The little one is urgent and must be processed immediately. The boss needs quick cash since we lost that shipment to that squealing bloody old coot. The big one is not so urgent but push her through anyway. Take care and no slip-ups, here, this is for getting rid of Johnson!"

Ray accepted the wad of notes offered by Gunther Berrimann, once again secreting the cash in an envelope he brought for the occasion.

"Great. Immediate cash is the way we like to do business. You'll get your stuff through, and pronto!" Ray and Gerry grinned expansively.

"Good to know the boss is impressed!" Gerry softly whispered.

"Yeah!" Gunther Berrimann made his exit from 'The River Café', happily content with the way he had replaced those two bunglers with a couple of reliable men; easily manipulated.

Ray and Gerry finished their lunches after Ray had notified Jason via his collar microphone that 'Berrimann' had left.

"Won't have to chase all over the warehouse for the two packages, Gerry." Ray told his friend.

"Yeah! I saw Berrimann stuff the paper into your pocket. Makes it so much easier to have the crate numbers."

"Well, come on you rotten conniving crook. Time to get back to work and 'run' some guns and drugs."

Ray slapped Gerry upon the back as they returned to the warehouse, eager to seek the next load of contraband. Within ten minutes of their return to work after lunch, both crates were located. Once again federal agents replaced the drugs with flour. The guns were delicately disabled by experts in that field, and then carefully repacked. Once again the trap was set; all awaited the next pick-up with eager anticipation.

Two men arrived at the warehouse to take delivery of one of the 'marked' crates, on behalf of Slimmery's Toy Factory. Both men were average build and were not of a very genial nature, implying that the job they were contracted to was more of an annoyance than an every-day job. As the van, their uniforms and the paperwork that they carried seemed official; the smaller crate of marked powder was entrusted to their care. Unknown to these men or indeed, to Ray and Gerry; a tracking device was secretly attached to the delivery van. The trap was triggered and the next step in this delicate manoeuvre was in place. Three S.I.O. agents discretely tracked the van at a safe distance. Even should they lose sight of their quarry, electronically it could be located. Lieutenant Ferguson and his staff were not surprised, when notified that the goods were by-passing the Moorabbin warehouse. A location towards the far eastern suburbs, in the lower reaches of the Dandenong Ranges; was where the van stopped. A small squad of agents kept the Moorabbin Toy Factory under surveillance, while the bulk of the strike force convoyed two kilometres behind the tracking vehicle.

"Lysle here Jason. The goods have entered the building, should we strike now?" Although speaking to his out of sight assistant, Lieutenant Ferguson shook his head.

"No. I want the big noises involved. Give them at least ten minutes. It will take that long for them to find out the stuff has been replaced. Then the bosses will come to see for themselves. Close in out of sight and then use your own discretion!"

A successful raid netted seven men, caught red-handed in the distribution centre of the east side cutting rooms. Vernon Chamberlain, a weedy little bald headed individual in his mid-forties, being the top man caught in the trap. He had been known to the C.I.D. but never convicted; due to the lack of evidence. His capture with the goods was a major blow to the drugs and gun-running cartel. Once again, the 'delivery boys', in this instance, Charlie Orso and Bernie Broccio; were not implicated, crying 'just deliverymen'. They walked free. Although the scam was successful, the S.I.O. was un-impressed.

"Damn the rotten luck!" Jason Ferguson thumped his desk in disappointment. "I was hoping that Schloss at least would have been there."

"But we nailed Chamberlain; we have been after him for a long while. And four of the other six won't be troubling us for some time. That is some sort of a win."

Sergeant Johnson grimly stated.

"Not good enough. I expected better. We needed Slimmery or Schloss at the very least. Anyway, I believe they are just pawns too; there is someone much higher than either of those two!" He drummed his fingers upon the desk, and then continued. "The really big boss is pulling strings from a position of high authority. Maybe even a member of the force – or even a government minister!"

Sergeant Johnson agreed.

"Yes, I believe you could be right. Then there is the Asian connection – the exporters – that may be where the directives come from!"

Jason appraised his underling with a frown.

"Crikey! I never gave that a thought. I assumed the top dog was here in Australia; you may well be right. Lysle, let's get our boys over there on to that line of thought; it may prove to be a winner. Well done!" Jason slapped his colleague upon the back.

"Flour! What do you mean, flour?"

Drew Slimmery seethed through clenched teeth, at Dermutt Schloss.

"It's a joke, right? I don't like that sort of million dollars joke Dermutt. Explain yourself!"

"The boys saw the stuff. Vernon tasted it and blew his top. Bernie and Charlie managed to get to the van before the raid began, that's how they were able to escape the trap. It was a set-up!"

Drew tried very hard to contain himself. He visibly shook and his small eyes exuded venom. A quick snatch at his pistol had Dermutt duck for cover behind the desk over which he had been addressing his superior. Three quickly discharged leaden messengers whizzed harmlessly over the stocky man's shoulders. A fourth tore into the flesh of the cowering pawn's upper arm. He screamed excuses as he clawed for his own concealed firearm. A well-directed shot hit Drew's gun hand, causing the weapon to be flung across the room. Dermutt shook with anger himself as he aimed his pistol squarely at his boss's upper chest. The two glared at each other across the desk, both bleeding from their wounds.

"Arsehole! Jumping to conclusions. Wasn't my fault, for all I know the bloody leak is coming through your office? How can you be so sure your line isn't tapped?"

"It ain't, I pay too well!" Drew breathed heavily, and then cooled. "All right so I made a mistake, put that thing away and let's get together on this; we can't afford to be at each other's throats!" Drew called to his secretary who was quivering in the outer office. "Get the first aid kit and wrap us up!" He brusquely ordered.

As the men were being attended, they began the elimination process.

"Johnson's out, but that doesn't mean he didn't set it up before your new men done him!" Drew pondered.

Dermutt did not believe that Arnold had sold them out, he knew the man to be dedicated to their cause as he was ever money-hungry. However, as the man was supposedly deceased, the heat could be taken off Dermutt by blaming him entirely.

"Yes, I reckon that must be it. You were right to dispose of him; very astute Boss!" Dermutt grovelled. Drew nodded absently, still not convinced.

"I'll go through my connections you do the same with yours. If you find a leak – exterminate it. What about those two new guys?" Dermutt shook his head confidently.

"Nah! They gloat over the money and it was no trouble for them to take out Johnson; did a good clean job of it too!" Drew appeared to agree, then queried.

"Ratt and Luntz?"

"Went interstate as you ordered. Well cashed up, even though they bungled things. They get their money too easy. We're safe there." Dermutt informed. "I'll double-check all of my connections and make sure I don't have the leak. I really think the feds have us bugged and that is the hole!"

"Probably." Drew drummed the top of his desk as was his wont, when thinking. "Get 'Doc' to fix your shoulder, and then send him in here. I'll have to do some thinking. I'll get in touch – dismissed!"

Dermutt Schloss was more angry than agitated when he left his immediate superior's office. The flesh wound in his shoulder stung like hell and he cursed Drew for flying off the handle as he did.

"Ruined a bloody good suit, damn him. Blast Ratt and Luntz for bungling all the time; made me look stupid. The boss doesn't have any confidence in me now. Bloody nincompoops!" Dermutt kicked a dustbin by which he was passing on the way to his vehicle. The contents spewed forth, causing a trail of litter as it rolled away.

"Dermutt!" Drew's voice sounded from afar.

Dermutt looked about and noticed Drew's head and shoulders protruding from a second-floor window.

"What?"

"Don't move the hardware, leave it where it is."

"Okay Boss!"

As the disgruntled man motored away, his thoughts were dark indeed. 'Drew must have the leak. I have just moved office and got new men who don't really know much. The boss should get his own house in order. The beggar ain't easy to work for, nowhere seems to be safe now, damn the rotten luck!' Dermutt drove to 'Doc' Lomax to have his wound properly attended. 'Doc' Lomax was at one time, a registered doctor but had been disqualified from medical practice through the distribution of unauthorised drugs. Now he made more money by servicing the medical needs of the underworld. The balding bespectacled little man went about his patch-up work with clinical precision. Drew Slimmery went there too and winced as 'Doc' patched his wounded right hand.

"You are extremely lucky Mister Slimmery." The 'Doctor' informed. "It appears that the slug sliced through the fleshy section between the index finger and thumb. The pistol took the full force of the bullet. Mostly lead shrapnel to pick out. You could have lost either or both digits."

"They all work, so I'll be sweet. Listen Doc, I need a word with a couple of my employees – truth drug – can you get that ready for when I deliver them to you?"

Drew casually asked.

"As you know Mister Slimmery, I am always ready and at your service. I have such items on hand, just give me the word. It would be better if you bring them to my 'workshop' you know!" The little doctor smiled.

"Sure, sure. Be a day or two though, I should say!" Drew smiled contentedly.

"Something real urgent has come up."

Dermutt Schloss spoke quietly to Ray as they conferred over coffee at 'The River Café', their agreed meeting place.

"The big boss wants a word with you and Gerry." He carefully eyed Ray as he spoke.

"Really! The big boss, and who might that be?" Ray casually asked.

"When you two meet him he may introduce himself. I'm not allowed to say."

"I see, why does he want to see us?"

"Probably to see who you are. He was impressed with the way you handled that Johnson coot; could be thinking of a promotion higher up the order. Who knows what he is thinking?" Ray nodded, as was his custom.

"Mister Berrimann!"

"Yes?"

"Before we front the boss, I want something cleared up."

"What?"

"When we took Johnson for a ride, he laughed at us. Johnson reckoned that your real name is Schloss; was he right?"
Smiling expansively, the man Ray and Gerry knew as Gunther Berrimann assented.

"Yeah! My real name is Schloss – Dermutt Schloss – I use the other on new recruits as a cover. Can't be too careful in our line of business. Now that you are with us, you need to know." The stocky little man then told the big foreman where the meeting with the 'big boss', was to take place. "Be there around seven-thirty this evening; right?"

"Glad you cleared that up, gives us more confidence to trust you!" Ray said.

Both men went about their business. Ray thought deeply upon the reason for the big wig to summon him and his mate to that evening's meeting. 'Has to be a catch in it somewhere I reckon. The man can't be just wanting to 'sus' us out and it's too soon for new men like us to be confidant's of the top brass. I have a premonition that it could spell bad news for Gerry and me. Must have an urgent word to Jason.' Ray arranged through his 'wire' to meet the Lieutenant within the hour.

"If they are legit about a promotion for you pair, that will be a huge benefit to us, but yes, I believe it is a 'set up'; can you spare an hour or so for me to arrange for Chief Flemming or Captain Vaughn to sit in on this?" Lieutenant Ferguson asked.

"Sure, have to; our very lives could well depend upon us getting this right. I'll have to ring through and have Gerry come here too. Hope no spies are watching on the warehouse floor; could be hard to explain both of us missing!"

"My worry is that I am getting civilians too deeply involved in this business." Jason fretted.

"She's Jake. We love it!" Ray was confident in his own ability. "Gerry thrives upon this 'cloak and dagger' work, so don't you worry about us!"

"Hmmmm!" Jason mused.

"Have to see if we can swear you in as deputies or something!"

CHAPTER FIVE

Drew Slimmery heaved an exasperated sigh.

"Damned if I can figure it out. We're definitely being sold down the river, but how? If it's not my connections and you can swear by your mob, then the 'feds' seem to be the only other option. I reckon they've planted a 'leak' in our system; but where?" His beady dark eyes bored into the man sitting opposite to him. "We'll have to set a trap. I'll have Sook Lin ship in a false consignment. For convenience we'll call it – er--!"

"Send it to Arnold, then the feds will notice it and think it's been on the water for a while." Dermutt suggested.

"Hey. That's an idea and I will have Lin label it, Curio's. That should get them interested. Right, I'll get the wheels turning and we'll soon know where the 'leak' is; meanwhile you double check your connections!"

Drew Slimmery dismissed his assistant with a slight wave of the hand. Dermutt scowled darkly as he was once again dismissed like an errant schoolboy. If only his boss knew what an enemy he was making for himself, of the man who used to be all for him. Charlie Orso and Bernie Broccio, the hirelings who posed as deliverymen for the supposed 'pure heroin', now free but under suspicion; were being 'ticked off' by Dermutt Schloss.

"I know it ain't your fault, but the boss has ordered that everyone is now to be checked out to make sure they are squeaky clean. Too many of our goods are getting tampered with; it ain't good for my image when things go astray like this!" Dermutt glared at his men with a venomous look. "You two were lucky not to get involved with the raid, now the boss is suspicious with everyone and I've got to check ém all out. I don't see how the two new men would be involved with the 'fuzz', but I got to keep an eye on them just the same. Now you two have got your orders so don't be knuckleheads like Joe and Bert; keep close tabs on those two at the warehouse but don't let them know you're doin' it. Okay, dismissed."

Dermutt waved them off with a snarl. When they left, he mumbled to himself.

"S'pose they'll muck it up as usual!"

"There are two new blokes tailing you fellows." The scarcely audible remark came from the man sweeping the gutter near Ray's car, as he parked it next to the fence of the car park.

"Thanks!" The big man whispered as he nonchalantly walked on by.

Speaking to Gerry at work, he casually mentioned the warning.

"We'll have to be careful not to raise their suspicions. Don't go looking; it'll be too obvious that we're on to them!"

"Gee. Did your mother teach you to suck eggs too?" Gerry chided. A matter-of-fact air of carefree reckless abandon on his features.

"Damn it, Gerry. This is serious you knucklehead!" Ray worried.

"Okay, point taken." Gerry calmly answered. "I'll be careful."

"Hmmpf, I'll believe that when I see it." They continued with their work.

That evening after letting their wives believe that they were required to be at a works meeting, the two intrepid customs men met Dermutt at a pre-arranged spot. They travelled in Dermutt's limousine to the 'workshop' of 'Doctor' Lomax. He received them cordially and ushered them into what appeared to be a waiting room. Presently he returned with a kidney dish upon which was a syringe and some methylated swabs.

"What is this?" Ray asked, suspiciously.

"Oh! I thought you knew. The top man is very fastidious about contamination and he insists all of the employees are vaccinated before he dares see them!" The 'Doctor' became very confidential. "Personally, I think it's a bit over the top, but he is the boss and we have to bow and scrape. It is quite harmless just a token gesture really, but the immunisation is beneficial. May I?"
He waited expectantly for their arms to be extended towards him. Ray obliged.

"I suppose we had better appease the man." They were injected.
The man who interviewed Ray and Gerry was rather dark and swarthy. He sported a flowing grey-specked full length beard and his dark eyes had a hypnotic effect. The questions he asked the pair under his power seemed to have no connection to reality at all. It was a topsy-turvey time for Ray and Gerry. Suddenly they found themselves being escorted to Dermutt's vehicle and whisked away back to their own cars.

"What happened?" Gerry asked of Ray when they were alone.

"It appears that we have been doped and did not get to see the real head of the cartel at all!" Ray explained.

"It is just as well Jason had his specialist Doctor to administer that antidote before we went there. I think we have been given a 'truth' drug. Goodness knows what we said but it must have satisfied them, because we are not dead!" Ray grimly stated.

A week passed and nothing untoward happened. No new shipments of contraband, hard or soft, were discovered by the diligent couple in the warehouse. At S.I.O. headquarters, Lieutenant

Ferguson was addressing his assistant, Detective Sergeant Carey. "All quiet on the home front Graeme. I reckon it is about time they landed another shipment."

"Yes, don't be surprised if it takes another form they are well aware that we are onto them; mark my words the next lot will be well disguised!"

"Unless they have already slipped one through."

"Don't think so. It is possible, but I have lots of confidence in our two plants. I doubt if much would escape their eagle eyes. They are good at what they do and I have good vibes about them." Jason offered.

"Are those two shadows still attached to them?" Graeme Carey asked.

"Seems like, Ray and Gerry are wearing them well. Agents Riley and Dean are watching the watchers like hawks, they won't have much chance to do Ray and Gerry any harm. God, I wish something would happen; this waiting has got whiskers on it!"

The telephone rang.

"Yes, Ferguson?"

"Detective Eugene Murphy, the security undercover at the warehouse is on his way to see you, Sir."

"What the devil does he want?"

"Can't say Sir. He says it is urgent."

"Thanks Jim." Jason turned to his assistant.

"What do you make of that? Eugene is coming here. Hope nothing is wrong!"

"Eugene! Isn't he the bloke we put in the store?"

"Yes. With instructions to keep an eye on our 'plants', something must have happened; get a squad ready!"

"Right!"

In ten minutes Eugene arrived he hurried into the room, knocking as he entered.

"Excuse me Jason, this could be important. The boys have unearthed a surprise delivery. It is addressed to Johnson – Arnold Johnson. They secretly had me slip out to notify you. We thought it best not to ring this one through in case they may be intercepting our lines!"

"Good thinking. Did they check if it is guns?"

"No Sir. Left it unmolested for us to decide."

"Great. Get back and cover them. I will have our squad move in tonight at eleven-thirty, tell Ray we will need him to move the night staff at that time!"

"X-rays show no guns and the dogs gave it a pass, Sir! The Sergeant smartly saluted as he reported. Jason gave the gaudy decorated crate another study, and then ordered the flying squad to disperse quietly. Back at his office, he and Detective Sergeant Carey were discussing this latest of moves.

"There is something rather smelly here. Why on earth would a crate be sent to Johnson when he is no longer about?"

"It may be a legitimate crate of junk. After all, he did manage a curio shop." Graeme noted.

"More of a junk shop, used as a dumping ground for anything illicit!" Jason mused. They both sat quietly, thinking.

"What was the return address?" Graeme asked. Jason referred to his notebook.

"Asian Antiques – common trade name and address – I am willing to bet it will not lead us anywhere." Jason nodded absently to himself. "It could be just a late arrival for Johnson. Then again, Johnson would have worried about it; unless he was unaware of it!"

"Eh?" Graeme pricked his ears.

"Well, look at it this way. The cartel addresses most of their stuff to Slimmery. He is now in the discard so far as deliveries are concerned. Maybe the cartel is trying a different ploy now. They could slip a consignment to Johnson and the delivery van would pick it up for Slimmery!"

"But the crate is clean!" Graeme expostulated.

"So it would seem." Jason thoughtfully drummed his fingers to help him concentrate.

"We think it's clean. Perhaps, just perhaps, they have come up with a way of disguising whatever their shipment is; a new lead-covered article made out to be an antique piece of bric-a-brac. That would confuse the x-ray machine and could also put the hounds off the scent."

"So, if it is not guns, it would have to be narcotics then!" Graeme said.

"We cannot take a chance; I suggest we wait for a pick-up that will tell us who ordered the stuff at least!" Jason agreed. "We will have to be careful with this one; we do not want egg all over our faces." He continued drumming.

"Yeah, this has to be carefully handled. It just may be a legitimate parcel of goods."

"Or a trap!" Graeme suggested.

"A trap. What makes you think that?" Jason shot a quick look at his assistant.

"Well, look at it from their point of view. We have come down heavy on a couple of their shipments. They must be wondering about a leak in their organization. It could be a ploy to find out where the leak is -!"

"Hey! Maybe you've got something there; now that is worth working on!"

A very clean, smart appearing yet innocuous looking delivery driver backed his van up to the outwards goods bay of the warehouse. He produced the correct papers for the pick-up of a crate of goods to go to a mister Arnold Johnson. Gerry assisted the man onto his van with the crate and had the papers signed. The delivery van left.

"What do you make of that?" Gerry asked Ray, as the vehicle disappeared from the loading bay.

"I don't know anymore; Jason just said 'let it go'!"

"I suppose Jason knows what they are doing, probably got a 'bug' in it." Gerry surmised.

Just before they were about to clock off, another van arrived and the driver asked for the same crate of goods.

"Sorry mate." Gerry said. "It has already been taken delivery of, I guess your boss got his lines crossed and sent two delivery trucks. It went about two hours ago!"

With a curse, the second driver departed.

"Now what is going on?" Gerry queried.

"That is strange. I had better let Jason know. I'll ring him up from a public 'phone on the way home." Ray worried.

"Ah good!" Jason replied to Ray's question. "That has put a spanner in their works. Don't worry Ray; we have it covered." He hung up on Ray.

The next day, Ray had an urgent meeting called by Dermutt, at their usual place in The River Café.

"We never took delivery of our goods. Our driver said it was already taken. Explain yourself!" The man was bristling with held in passion.

"Now hang on a bit. I don't know your drivers, they are always different. How am I supposed to know if they are the legitimate pick-ups?"
Ray was not to be bullied. He frowned at Dermutt.

"Our man said the goods were gone a couple of hours before he arrived."

"Yes, I was told that a second van came for the goods designated to Arnold, but I believed the second van was just a 'double up'; it often happens!" Ray said, slightly peeved.

"Did the first van have any distinguishing names on it?" Dermutt asked, rather agitatedly.

"I didn't see it, my second-in-command did the dispatch, but the papers had a Toy Factory heading of some sort. Does that help?" Ray asked.

"Toy factory! Sounds like someone is pulling a fast one here. My boss runs a toy business and his bus was the second one; not the first. There is something fishy here. Ah well, I daresay you weren't to know. I will have another word to my boss!"

"You handled that well." Jason applauded upon being informed of what had transpired.

"Seeing that it was an impromptu meeting and we did not have you wired, thanks for coming in and letting us know!"

"Then you're not mad about the two delivery trucks?" Ray asked, incredulously.

"Not at all. You see, the first van was a 'plant' of ours. We need to confuse them about the 'leak'. By thwarting them like this, they will think that they have opposition; another cartel trying to undermine them. I think we will have them guessing!"

Jason was smugly confident.

"Oh well, I dare say you know what you are doing."

"You had better get back to your wife; you have been having a good few late nights lately. Don't want her to be unduly worried for you. Keep up the good work – and thanks!" Jason applauded. Ray left.

"Just rubbish sir!" The sergeant reported to Jason. "No sign of drugs or guns and it has lots of worthless bric-a-brac neatly packed. We replaced everything as it was and even the seals have been remodelled. To all intents and purposes, the goods have not been tampered with."

"Thank you Sergeant!" Jason turned to his subordinate. "Well. Any ideas Graeme?" Graeme Carey stroked his chin as he thought deeply.

"Nothing springs to mind. Unless we return it to the Warehouse!"

"Return it?" Jason expostulated. Graeme nodded, as he elaborated.

"We could just say that it was picked up by mistake – pretend that it was a different Toy Factory – with a similar name. Say they were expecting Pogo Sticks and this one could not possibly be theirs because it is too small!"

Jason gave the matter some thought, and then absently nodded.

"Yes. I suppose that would work. We will get Ray to give the next delivery-van from Slimmery's a message about its return!"

Ray and Gerry were in The River Café, Ray was wired, and they were in urgent consultation with Dermutt Schloss.

"Because it is addressed to Arnold and he is gone, we thought it may be for you!"

Ray emphasised.

"So you reckon the first van picked it up by mistake?" Dermutt asked.

"I reckon so. I was the one who gave it to the driver; his papers seemed to be in order; so I let him have it!" Gerry intervened.

"So now the package is back in the warehouse?" Dermutt muttered.

"Yeah. It has not been opened either, they said they realized it was not theirs because they are expecting Pogo Sticks. The crate is too small to accommodate them, so they just returned it. We looked around and soon found the parcel of Pogo Sticks!" Ray frowned.

"Okay. I will send a pick-up for the crate. Good work!" Dermutt left.

Drew Slimmery was in deep thought. He drummed his fingers as was his custom.

"Are you positive that the seals were unbroken?"

"So our new receiving man said. He checked that out first. It appears that it was an apparent mix-up."

"And you say that your two new men notified you of its return as soon as it came back?" Dermutt gave a nod of assent.

"So I think that proves those two are on the ball and are working for us!" He stressed.

"Yes. It would appear so. Evidently the warehouse is not where the leak is; so it must be from inside the cartel somewhere. The Feds must have a plant here."

Drew surmised. Dermutt scratched his chin thoughtfully.

"What about Larry's boys. Do you think they have anything to do with this 'leak'?"

"Nah! Wouldn't be them, they are just 'stand overs', make their money from the rackets – bully-boy tactics, there is no worries there!" Drew answered as he appeared to suddenly come to a conclusion. "The Richmond storage has already been raided – transfer the Johnson crate there – unopened. We will see if that gets a nibble!"

It was a couple of days later and Dermutt unexpectedly called on his boss. "It had better be urgent; I have a dinner appointment in half an hour!" Drew Slimmery growled.

"Yes, it is!" Dermutt blurted. "I told you my new men were good. They informed me just a while ago that the Feds are planning a raid on the Richmond place again!"

"What! How would they know?" Drew suspiciously asked.

"Appears that the Feds made a lightning swoop on the warehouse and Gerry happened to overhear a couple of the Feds discussing it. Something about 'Richmond plant now'. They rang me just now and I came as quick as I heard. Didn't want to risk the 'phone!"

"How the hell did the Feds know?" Drew asked. "The leak must be in the Richmond camp!"

"Dunno. Just thought you had to know!" Dermutt grovelled.

"Okay, thanks. It's probably too late to warn them now, it does not matter anyway; the place is clean!"

"We did as you instructed Jason. The warehouse and then the Richmond store. We confiscated the Johnson crate as ordered and their excuse was, 'We thought it was for us'!"

"So they do not want us to know there was a connection between the cartel and Johnson. Hmmm, that is interesting."

"Do you think that they knew what was in the crate was just worthless goods?" Graeme asked.

"Definitely. I think it was just an elaborate ploy to trip our plants up, supposing they suspected we have one." Jason smiled. "I guess that they are worried now that the 'plant or leak', is in the Richmond place!"

"What will our next move be?" Graeme asked.

"We urgently need to locate the top guy in this racket. I think we will have to get above Dermutt somehow. We have to get Ray promoted higher up in the organization. Get your thinking cap on; this will have to be good!" Jason stated, firmly.

It was a Saturday afternoon. Ray and Cindy were discussing whether they would have an afternoon at the beach or just stay at home and relax.

"But we can just as easily relax at the beach as here!" Cindy called from the laundry.

"When I put this lot in the dryer, I am finished; so there is nothing stopping us."

"Ahhh well, I suppose --??" Ray began, as the doorbell sounded.

"Get that dear; I am busy for a bit." Cindy called. Ray was already at the door.

"Yes? Oh, you look like--!" He began. He was interrupted.

"Collie, of the 'Special Branch', Jason requests you come to this address!"

'Collie' showed his badge and passed a card to Ray.

"On our day off?" Ray queried.

"It is very important." The detective insisted.

"Oh well, I suppose I had better." Ray had to console Cindy and beg her forgiveness once more. "I will make it up to you tonight Sweet. We'll go out for dinner!"

"Here we go again. I will be glad when this business is over and done with!" Cindy sighed.

When Ray had made sure that his car was locked, another car pulled up behind his.

"Gerry!" He said, surprised. "You too. What do you think this is all about?"

"Darned if I know. I thought you would tell me!" Gerry puzzled.

"Well, let us go in and find out!"

They entered the premises together. Lieutenant Ferguson was there accompanied by Captain Vaughn. The two visitors were asked to sit down while Captain Vaughn remained standing; he hovered over the two civilians.

"Sorry to disturb you both on your day off but this is an urgent matter." He began. "As you two are getting very involved in this cartel, we think you need better protection from our side of the fence. We therefore deem it appropriate that you both be sworn in as probationary officers, for you own protection. Are you in agreement?"

Ray, with raised eyebrows, looked at Gerry. He had a whimsical grin on his face.

"If you think that is necessary, why not?" Ray spoke for them both.

And so the two, with bibles in hand, were sworn in as probationary officers.

CHAPTER SIX

Fatty Burns was a rather obese man. His balding head had just a wisp of sandy coloured hair about the back and his nose was plump and red. No doubt he hit the bottle a lot. When he arrived at the airport he had with him two uncomplimentary companions, Joe Ratt and Bert Luntz. The three furtively slipped into a 'hired' car and were whisked away to an inner suburban address. When they were settled, Joe appeared at the home of Dermutt and was secreted inside. Shortly thereafter, Joe remained there while Dermutt called upon Drew Slimmery. Plans were made and Dermutt eventually returned to his home and gave Bert his orders. The underling hurried back to his new boss with the information he had been given by Dermutt. Fatty Burns swung into action and began the organization of a Pizza Parlour in a busy suburban street. He hired new staffs that were cooks and deliverers and nothing more. After the opening of the business, when all due checks were made, it was left alone by the authorities and by-law officers. To all intents and purposes, it was a thriving new business; doing well.

"I do not understand it at all." Jason muttered to himself as he studied his books. "It just does not add up. Why all of a sudden is there no activity in the warehouse or on the streets. We seem to be missing something somewhere?"

Graeme looked up from his own work at the murmurings of his immediate superior.

"Missing something?" Jason sat back and conversed with thumb and finger on his chin.

"Yes. There just is no sense to it at all. Why should everything be so quiet – we are being left out of the activity somewhere?" Graeme offered.

"We hit the importers hard; they must have just about gone crazy when their shipments were being seized. Do you think they have found another loop-hole to get their stuff through?"

"That is about the only answer. Ray has reported that Slimmery has stopped his deliveries; he has not had a thing of any suspicious nature to report. To all intents, Slimmery does not even exist anymore!" Jason went back to studying papers. Graeme offered.

"Must have decided to stop all work at his Toy Factory and started a new venture!"

"No doubt, but what and where?" Jason queried. He rang Ray Cress.

"Now that you are recruited to the underworld, we believe that you will be safe from attack for a while; therefore the consensus of opinion is that there is no need to have your families covered day and night." Jason confided to his two undercover men.

Ray nodded agreement.

"Yes. The heat seems to be off now that they think we are working for Dermutt. But I am suspicious that we are not being used by the cartel anymore!"

Ray said a note of misgiving in his voice. It was detected by Jason.

"Look, if we hear anything that might even remotely be construed as threatening; we will cover you and yours in a flash. We are keeping the connections of the cartel under close scrutiny; Charlie and Bernie still have a 'tail' and Dermutt Schloss too is being monitored" Jason sounded very sure of his connections.

"Gee, I hope you are right. But the cartel would not just stop their activities overnight. They must be active in another area. You will let us know if anything untoward eventuates?"

"Of course. Trust me, we will find out what is happening and you will be informed."

Ray left it at that and returned home to tell Cindy that all was well. Detective Sergeant Ronald Shell, of the local C.I.D. called in to Lieutenant Ferguson's office.

"How is the cartel going? Got any new leads?" He asked after salutations were dispensed with.

"Seems to have pulled its head in since we have made a few raids. They appear to have gone underground." Jason worried.

"Well I may have something for you to go on with. My blokes are ever alert as you know. One of my uniform boys spotted someone the other day, someone who went interstate; Bertram Luntz! I just thought it may be important for you to know he is back."

"Luntz eh? Was that other no-good with him – er – Ratt; Joseph Ratt?" Jason showed a little interest.

"Only got word of Bert. He went into a betting shop, near the racecourse. Suppose the other scoundrel would be about somewhere. He was not sighted." Ron grinned.

"Thanks for that, it may be just the lead we're looking for; near the racecourse you say?"

"So the uniformed man reckons. He thought it may be important for you to know who is about!"

"Thanks, I will have some of the staff 'sus' him out. It just may lead us somewhere!"

When the next race meeting was held, an undercover man watched the said betting shop for a couple of days. It was not until the third day that Bert Luntz was espied going in to place a bet. He was followed back to his new residence. A permanent watch was put in place.

"I dare say that Luntz is up to no good, but we can not pin that on him. So far there has been no sighting of his side-kick, Ratt; they may not be working together now." Jason said to his fellow worker. Graeme frowned at him.

"Just because Joe has not been seen does not mean that they have parted. Once a team is made up, it is usually best to keep it together."

"Neither of the two has been seen at the Factory or at Richmond, of course that may be because they were sent to Sydney. This new address they seem to be at – it is clean so far as reports go; may be they have turned over a new leaf?" Jason smiled, not meaning a word of it.

"Maybe. But then, I have not seen a porcupine fly either!" Graeme quipped, sarcastically.

Ray Cress was watching some children playing a game of soccer at a public park. An unmarked police car pulled up in the car park and a tall officer got out. He came towards Ray. "G'day." Ray said looking attentively about to see that the officer was not followed.

"Why all this secrecy, has something important happened?" Jason looked keenly at the other big man.

"I don't know. It just may be nothing but I was suspicious and I thought we had better be sure than sorry later!" Ray cryptically replied.

"What is the problem? Have you found something?" Jason gently probed.

"Now I am only guessing but there seems to be an anomaly. Gerry found a new consignment of goods that does not seem to add up. It comes from that Asian port that Slimmery uses but it is addressed to a Pizza place and there seems to be an extra-ordinary large amount of it just for a small Pizza place."

"But just because it comes from the same port of call that Slimmery uses, does not mean that it has anything to do with Slimmery!" Jason explained.

"But this is supposed to be fine grained flour! Why would a small Pizza place import flour when it may be obtained cheaper at home?"

Jason was silent for a minute, analysing this latest piece of information.

"I think you are grabbing at straws but I will get the sniffer dogs on to it just the same. It is probably a legitimate transaction for some exotic food-house. Still, we can not afford to miss a trick at the moment and things are a bit quiet. Thanks for trying anyhow, the squad will make a raid tonight; just routine."

"So you believe it is just an ordinary delivery?"

"Who knows, there is no law that says flour cannot be imported, I don't think." Jason airily said, as he waved goodbye to Ray. "We'll cover it just the same. Good job Ray; it is better to be on the safe side."

He drove away leaving Ray to lean on the rail watching the children at play. 'I still think it is very suspicious'! Ray thought to himself. 'There is no way a small business would be bothered to import that much flour. It is not economical'. He went back home to his lovely wife Cindy. Dermutt Schloss met with Ray and Gerry at 'The River Café', where Dermutt was saying that the money would have to be halved, now that they were not needed to hurry shipments through.

"You see, since we have been 'hit' so much, we have had to stop the shipments. You won't be dropped altogether, we still may need you. But until there is some work for you, the payments will be lower."

"Aw gee! That's a blow; we were getting to like the easy money from you. You sure we can't do anything?" Ray sounded peeved.

"Look, I'm sure it's just temporary, I will let you know when the imports start again!" Dermutt calmed.

"We can give you lots of information – like when the dog squad comes in – they 'hit' us last night. A crate of flour for some Pizza joint or other."

"Eh. What's that?" Dermutt pricked up his ears. "What Pizza joint?"

"Oh just a new place that opened. The dogs found it on a routine inspection. They are always coming in unexpectedly!" Ray tried to sound off-hand.

"Bloody mongrels!" Dermutt angrily blurted.

"What has you so upset? It is only a small-time business!" Ray looked surprised.

"Never mind, I have to go – look, I will not stop your payments just yet. Keep us informed on any dog raids!" Dermutt hurried away.

Ray and Gerry smiled at each other when Dermutt had left.

"Bingo! I believe we hit a raw nerve. Your suspicions turned out to be very correct. Let us notify the big bloke about this latest escapade."

Gerry had a smile as big as a football ground.

"See! I am not just a pretty face!" He plumped his chest.

Ray leaned over for a closer look.

"Huh? No - you're not either!"

The foreman dodged a paper napkin hastily screwed up and thrown at him.

"Get back to work you loafer. Do I have to do all the hard jobs for you?" Gerry retorted. Ray hurried out.

Lieutenant Ferguson was talking with Captain Vaughn.

"The place was clean. Not a sniff in the joint, maybe we stopped the first shipment!" Jason's disappointment was showing.

"Don't think so. It has been too long since our last confiscation, they evidently do not use the premises for delivery. Maybe they just take orders there and the deliveries are made elsewhere?" Captain Vaughn suggested.

"Could be but it is not logical. Usually the users want it there and then – in and out – that way they get the stuff immediately; no mucking about!"

"Yes. There must be some other answer. I would say that there is definitely another 'cutting room' about some where, they don't even distribute the finished product from the Pizza place!"

"No, the dogs would have picked up a scent then!" Jason confirmed. "Perhaps we should have let that crate go through instead of confiscating it?"

"No. I believe you were right to take this one; we do not want the cartel to get suspicious of our two in there. This way there is no 'sameness' about the different shipments!" Captain Vaughn was adamant.

A very flustered Dermutt Schloss was informing his boss.

"I got it first-hand from my two on the payroll there. I tried to cut them down a bit and they said that they could tell us when a dog raid was on. Ray mentioned that just the other night the dogs found some stuff in a shipment to some Pizza place or other, I never told them about our shop. They did not know it was our goods!"

Drew, very red in the face and fuming, remained calm.

"So it's still in the warehouse?" His question was hostile.

"They are probably waiting for us to pick it up!" Dermutt snivelled.

Drew was very quiet, he thoughtfully put his head in his hands and sat there thinking.

"Fore warned is fore armed, we will have to let it simmer for a bit. Blast the Feds and their rotten mongrels!" He clenched his hands tightly. "We will have to find another way of getting the stuff in, it is getting too expensive losing these shipments!"

Joe Ratt was watching a light aircraft as it came in to land at a country aerodrome within forty kilometres of the main metropolis. This was an unusual aircraft in that it had floats attached as an undercarriage. The floats were raised and the landing wheels were lowered for the small plane to come to rest on the grassy strip. Joe quickly manoeuvred the small panel van he was driving, into a position close to the hatch of the plane. The pilot assisted with a package to have it safely secreted into the van. Joe waved as he drove away. Some fifteen kilometres back towards the city proper, the van entered a farm property where the package was delivered. Joe and the van returned to his new residence. Dermutt Schloss was seen to enter these premises at a late night time and stayed for about an hour, after which the plain-clothed detective witnessed him leaving. It was a further fifteen minutes later that Bert Luntz returned to these same premises.

"So!" Jason answered his telephone. "We have the old firm in action again. Joe Ratt and Bert Luntz with Dermutt Schloss all at the one address together?" He said into the speaker. "You say that Joe is now driving a small panel van eh! You do not happen to know where he came from."

"No Sir, just that he came back in it, I checked the registration and it has been hired!" Detective Murphy answered.

"What say you nick over to the warehouse and ask Ray if that van has been there to pick anything up; there could be a connection!"

"First thing in the morning Sir." Jason replaced the receiver and turned to his assistant.

"Everything seems to be new lately. That Joe and Bert are back is nothing in itself, what is interesting is that they now have a panel van and that although Joe and Bert are living at the same house, they do not seem to be working together. Bert is seen at a betting premises and Joe is driving a hired van somewhere up bush!"

"Do you think that is where the new cutting room is?" Graeme asked.

"It would not surprise me!" Jason thoughtfully admitted.

"At last our connections seem to be in order!" Drew thankfully breathed a sigh of relief. "The new system is working well. No hiccups and the stuff is getting through."

"Yeah. I got to hand it to you Boss that was a brainy thought of yours. We are not getting stuffed around with by that 'leak' and bringing Ratt and Luntz back with their new work is proving a good choice!" Dermutt lapped up their successes with gusto.

"What about the Pizza joint. Do we still retain that?" He asked, rather tentatively.

"Yes. I do not see it being used as we first thought but given time and a clean slate, it may yet be a viable asset. We could still use the place as an outlet for the finished product. Keep the staff on and keep it 'clean' for the time being!"

Dermutt left his boss with a satisfied smirk on his face. 'Hope this time the deliveries keep coming through, then we can forget the warehouse'. He thought to himself. At his office, Dermutt was checking with one of the two men he had ordered to keep a watch on Ray and Gerry.

"I do not think it is much use keeping tabs on those two in the warehouse any longer. They easily moved through a grilling at Doc's and they seem to be working for us okay, the Boss reckons that we could be wasting resources trying to find fault when there is no fault to find. He wants me to put you two to better use. Joe is doing pick-ups; Bert is on the betting shop so the big bloke says I should have you two pushing a bit of the stuff. How about 'hitting' the High School. The rich kids can find 'dough' when they need it – get Bernie and have a go there, Charlie!"

"Yep! Sounds like a good spot to try; probably when they are leaving school to go home would be the best time. Once we have made a contact, word of mouth should sell the stuff!" Charlie agreed.

"Right. Get to it and don't get caught!" Dermutt ordered.

"Still quiet on the airwaves?" Jason asked his radio operator. "Yes Sir. Nothing other than the usual drivel, although there is some talk of a 'Hewie', whoever he is; I just haven't worked him out yet. I think he has flown in from interstate. There was a call to Dermutt from this 'Hewie' who said he just arrived. Said he flew in last Tuesday, I believe that is where Joe took the van; probably to pick him up!"

"Hmm! A new bloke for us to chase up and keep an eye upon!" Justin worried.

Later, at his desk, Jason was discussing the intervention of this new player in the puzzle with Graeme.

"What the connection 'Hewie' has with the cartel could be interesting. That he has 'flown in' seems to indicate that he has been recruited from somewhere or other, but to what end?" Graeme suggested.

"Maybe he is a 'heavy' from an interstate branch of the cartel?" The Lieutenant looked at his assistant in a pensive way.

"Yes, maybe. The streets are still quiet so far as any influx of new drugs is concerned. We seemed to have closed them down temporarily!"

"Excuse me Sir!" An undercover detective popped in to say. "We are getting reports from the uniformed branch that there appears to be an outbreak of new 'hits' about the vicinity of the High School. One of the students has reported that a stranger has been accosting them after school with cheap drugs."

"Really! A student? Must be a Good Samaritan, they usually stick together." Jason wondered.

"This lad was very angry about it, seems that his mother was addicted to heroin and it tore the family apart. He did not leave an address; wanted to remain anonymous!"

"Thank goodness some of the kids have a sense of responsibility. Thank you Senior!"

Jason turned to Graeme.

"I wonder if this is connected to the cartel – seems suspiciously like it?"

"No doubt." His junior replied. "Perhaps that is why this 'Hewie' came down. A new face and all that!"

"Could be – then again, Dermutt would have no need to go to the expense of getting in a new player just to 'push' the stuff. There are ample people here already for that. No, I believe this 'Hewie' is a little more high profile than a mere 'pusher'!" Jason asserted, with conviction.

Ray and Cindy were at Gerry's house. Natalie beamed with delight that they called in.

"Ah. Now don't tell me you two love-birds got tired of your own company!" She teased. Tiffany, the four-year-old daughter, was tugging at Ray's trousers leg. Cindy responded to the teasing.

"No, we were just wondering how the other folk live who are weighed down with children!"

The tugging persisted. Ray, slightly amused, looked down at the cause of his discomfort.

"Yes Tiffany, What is it?"

"I got a new dolly, do you want to play wiv it Uncle Way?" Ray took the offered doll.

"Yes, that is a nice doll; thank you but I think she wants her mummy."

He patted it and handed it back. Tiffany ran off, delighted that she was taken notice of. The older daughter was not to be left out. Six year old Jo-Anne butted in.

"I got a better doll than Tiffy's; mine closes her eyes when I put her to bed!"

Ray also accepted her doll and did his duty as an 'Uncle' to the little girl. Gerry replied to the soft raillery.

"Ah! You poor suckers are just jealous. You do not see the cute little faces when they are asleep. It makes the noise all worth it!"

"Well. What have you planned for today? You would not care to come on a picnic with us; I suppose?" He looked happily at his friends. Astonished, they looked to each other.

"Hey! That is not a bad idea!" Gerry agreed. "What do you reckon Sweetie, dress the kids in some rompers and we can let them run about the oval. It would be a break for you; get you out of the house and all that. What about it?" Cindy added.

"There is no need for you to pack any lunch. I have already scraped up enough for us adults. You only have to grab some bits and pieces for the girls; and some drinks for them!" Cindy offered.

"Golly! You are twisting our arms aren't you? Sure, we would love to. Give us half an hour to get the kids dressed and put something together for them!" Natalie urged.

"Can I help with the girls?" Cindy asked.

Soon the two vehicles were travelling along the freeway to a little country town. Jo-Anne was allowed to ride with Ray and Cindy, where she was talkative and happy.

"There is the little picnic area I had in mind." Ray nodded the direction with his head.

"There seems to be an air strip here. There are a couple of planes about." Cindy noted.

"Yes." Ray explained. "That is why this picnic spot is so unspoiled by housing. The developers are not allowed to build close to an air strip."

"Are Natalie and Gerry still following?" Cindy asked as she turned in her seat belt to try and see for herself. Ray glanced in the rear-view mirror.

"Yes, they did not miss the turn-off. They are right behind us!" He assured her.

Soon the two cars pulled alongside each other under the shade of a leafy bush.

"Hey! This looks to be an ideal spot. There is a nice table and seats where we can keep a good watch on the girls. May even see a couple of planes touch down from here!"

Ray said as he asked Gerry if they thought this spot would do.

"Oh yes!" Natalie answered for her man. "This is a lovely spot. Aren't you glad I talked you in to coming on this picnic?"

"Just for that, you can have your daughter back." He ruffled the little girl's hair with a smile.

They were all sitting down around the picnic table, when Natalie frowned as she asked Gerry.

"What on earth is that strange looking aircraft?"

Natalie pointed out the one in question. All looked to the direction indicated.

"That is just a seaplane Sweetie; you do not see many of them out in the bush like this. They mostly stick to the bays and rivers." Gerry advised.

"That is why it looks so strange." Ray added. "Those queer contraptions on the undercarriage are called 'pontoons', to let the craft float on the water!"

"Oh!" Natalie pouted. "I have never seen one before that is why I thought it looked odd."

"Yes, come to think of it; it is odd that it should be way up bush like this?" Ray queried.

"Come on Ray. Let's go play 'keepings off' with the girls." Gerry picked up the ball they brought along for the purpose and called the girls to catch him. Ray followed.

Drew Slimmery played host to Dermutt Schloss. An oily smile permeated his somewhat bloated face. He poured a glass of red wine for himself and did likewise for Dermutt.

"At last the shipments are getting through and it appears that the finished stuff is having an airing at the schools." Drew grinned expansively at his underling.

"Yeah. I knew those two would be good for something!" Dermutt took a sip of wine and asked.

"How did you get on to Hewie?"

Drew bored into the face of his second-in-command for a minute, and then shrugged.

"Ah. It does not matter, suffice to say we have him and the goods are getting through!"

CHAPTER SEVEN

Lieutenant Ferguson happened along to the Warehouse with his assistant, Sergeant Carey.

"What a surprise to see you two here. Aren't you taking a risk of 'blowing' our cover?" Ray asked. Jason shook his head.

"No, I doubt if there is any more need for us to be worried on that score. The cartel seems to have a more reliable new source of getting the goods through now!"

"Once bitten twice shy." Ray recited.

"I am afraid so, we seem to have scared them off using the import areas. They just seem to have got a new means of getting the drugs and guns in. I was hoping that you may have some idea of how imported goods can by-pass the warehouse. Do you have any inkling, I am afraid we are getting no where since it has dried up. We were so close to getting at the big guy too!" Graeme asked. "Do you know of another importer that they may be using; some little insignificant out-of-the-way sleazy joint?"

Ray pursed his lips and shook his head.

"Larson's or Jander's? No, they would be too small. The type of shipments the cartel has would be noticeable at a furriers or timber peoples business. Could they be shipping them in to an independent pier? I seem to have read somewhere that goods like drugs were dropped off outside the heads and then they were picked up by a smaller vessel." Ray thoughtfully suggested.

"Yes and even skin divers have been used. Perhaps something of the sort is happening here. They are getting the stuff in; we know that!" Graeme said.

Jason bid the two would-be sleuths goodbye with a parting suggestion.

"Do not be surprised if suddenly you come across another shipment. The cartel may be getting their goods through now but there is always the chance of a slip-up!"

At lunch the two storemen were discussing the morning's events.

"Jason appears to have taken off the under covers. Do you feel any safer without people keeping an eye out for you?" Gerry asked his superior.

"It doesn't seem to have made any difference. I did not think they were necessary in the first place!" Ray said with conviction. "I wonder if Dermutt still has his two keeping an eye on us."

"Nah! We got a clean bill of health with that 'truth drug' the cartel hit us with. They would not be wasting money with that line of thought anymore!" Gerry was adamant.

"Be on your guard just the same!" Ray advised. "These are ruthless people. You just can not take them for granted."

Back at work, Gerry pulled Ray aside up an aisle where no one would notice them.

"Hey. What's got into you?" Ray admonished. Gerry whispered.

"I think I have found another shipment!"

"Are you sure?"

"Seems like. Aisle twenty two shelf three, you go and have a look!"

Ray casually walked out of the aisle where Gerry had forced him in and with papers in hand, tried to inconspicuously to assess the goods in doubt. He circled back to Gerry.

"Go on you duffer. That is a legitimate crate of toys, it is addressed to Albert Johnsen – not Johnson – and that bloke's name is Albert – not Arnold. We have had a crate of toys before for that address, different Toy Works. No; that is not suspicious just as well to be alert though."

Ray slapped his co-worker on the back.

"Keep up the sleuthing" he said, ungrammatically "you may yet make it to constable!"

"Shush you dopey drongo, someone may hear you!" Gerry frowned. "You told me to be alert. What about you?"

"Point taken, come on, let us earn our pay!"

"Detective Lynton to see you Sir" The man ushered the radio operator through the door.

"Yes Jim?" Jason asked.

"It may be nothing but we are grabbing at straws. I just picked up a conversation between Joe Ratt and Dermutt Schloss; they were discussing when the next 'payload' was due."

"And - ?" Jason waited.

"Dermutt said on Tuesday!" Jim Lynton took a deep breath, and then announced his coup-de-gras.

"Joe asked what time should he meet Hewie and was told seven-thirty. But here is the important part; Joe said 'I dunno how he can land that thing with them funny contraptions on it'!"

"Ah! So when he 'flew in', he actually did it as a pilot. That is interesting!" Jason stroked his chin as he frowned.

"You missed the point Sir, 'them funny contraptions on it', that is the most interesting part!" Jim Lynton stressed.

"Funny contraptions?" Jason queried. "I wonder to what he was referring?"

"It may be insignia of some sort." Lysle suggested.

"No. I do not think that would be detrimental to flying an aircraft." Jason worried. Graeme came up with an idea.

"Could it be flags or a grappling device of some sort?"

His superior turned to him, shaking his head.

"Flags maybe but why would they have flags? It would identify the aircraft but they would not wish to be noticed, no not flags. Grappling device – maybe – but then the 'plane would be too noticeable. It is a bit of a puzzle!"

"Do you think we should monitor the air terminal Jason?" Graeme asked. Jason thoughtfully pondered this latest avenue of concern. "It will not come in at a major air port; I believe we should look further a field. One of the nearby country strips would be more logical. There are so many of them in a wide vista of country that is the trouble!" Again Jason drummed his fingers on the desk, a sure sign he was troubled. "If the cartel now has a new means of getting the drugs etcetera in, they will have no further need of the warehouse!" He informed his assistant. Graeme nodded his agreement.

"A pity that. We had a good thing going there for a couple of weeks. Nearly paid off too!"

"So! I reckon that the shipments have been changed, possibly to a coastal type vessel, dropped off some where along the coast; maybe at a deep water jetty where they are picked up and delivered to somewhere that this 'Hewie', can fly them in to a country airstrip! What do you think?" Jason looked triumphantly to Graeme."

"Sounds logical!" His assistant agreed.

"Have to get Riley and Dean to 'tail' this Ratt on Tuesday morning when he leaves to pick up the goods." Jason said. "With a bit of luck he will lead us right to the airstrip the cartel is using!"

"That is the go. Maybe we will be successful this time." Sergeant Carey hoped.

"Will you organize them for me? Make sure that they get into position early, this may be our only chance." He left it in his assistant's hands and went about his duties.

The telephone sounded at Headquarters. Jason, with a grin, picked up the handset.

"Agent Riley Sir. It is just on noon and there has been no sign of Joe Ratt or his off-sider, Sir!"

"Nothing at all?"

"No Sir. We have had the premises under surveillance since midnight and we are getting tired, but not a sign of those two. Dermutt came out and went to the corner shop. He returned with the paper; that is all Sir." Detective Riley sounded as if he had a boring time.

"I will put Fox and Carruthers on to take over from you. Just keep an eye out and your relief will be there soon!"

"Yes Sir." Jason turned to Detective Carey.

"Damn. I believe we have been duded, I am sure we have missed them. They must have picked up the stuff by now; I wonder where the snivelling hound was to have eluded our chaps like that?" Jason cursed the rotten luck.

Ray's mobile 'phone interrupted him while he was indulging in some catch-up paperwork.

"Hello, you have Ray, can I help you?"

"It is Jason. Look, I seem to have missed a connection somewhere. Have you or Gerry been contacted by Schloss in recent days?"

"No." Ray answered, shaking his head although his caller could not see him. "The cartel seems to have forgotten about us. I guess we are redundant now."

"No, I did not think you would be used now – I just had to check. We are at a dead end. Even Joe Ratt has eluded us."

"What, is he back?"

"Yes. No need to get all of a dither about him. He seems to be doing pick-ups from the country somewhere!"

"The country?" Ray asked. "What would the cartel be doing in the country? Do you think they have a 'cutting room' there?" It was Jason's turn to shake his head.

"Anything is possible with this lot. But we think he is their go-between. They appear to be dropping the stuff off outside the heads and then a light 'plane brings it to an outback airstrip. We suspect Joe of getting it from there and delivering it up country somewhere else!"

"Hey! They wouldn't be using a seaplane would they?" Ray said with enthusiasm.

"A seaplane?" Jason queried. "What makes you mention a seaplane?"

"We were having a picnic – Gerry's family and mine – up near that airstrip forty kilometres away on the lower slopes of the ranges. And guess what we saw there – a seaplane. It had those attachments on, you know, pontoons. We thought it very odd that one of them would be at a country airstrip. They usually frequent bays and waterways."

"Oh. That is interesting. Thanks Ray!" Jason replaced his telephone and did some very heavy cogitation. 'If they are using a seaplane, then it is possible to pick the stuff up while they are on the water. They will not need a customs warehouse and even the risk of a pier or jetty is negated. Yes; now that is worth working upon'. He called to his assistant

"Oh Graeme, get here, we have some heavy organizing to do!"

The following day, after agents Riley and Dean were properly rested; they were sent to the country airstrip where Ray and Gerry reported seeing the aircraft with the pontoons attached. Although they kept the airfield under surveillance for hours, no sighting of an aircraft with pontoons appeared.

"Could be hidden inside a hanger!" Dean said to Riley.

"Yes, that is possible. We can't afford to be seen poking about, Jason said not to be noticed." Riley emphatically stated.

A fourteen year old boy rode up to the fence on a cycle. He watched an aeroplane taxi across the field to get ready for take-off. He stood still, very interested.

"Psstt!" Riley quietly signalled to him.

The boy looked to the sound and saw the two men motioning for him to come over to them. He shook his head from side to side, indicating that he was not coming. The boy grabbed his cycle and started to leave.

"Hey Son – police!" Detective Riley flashed his badge.

The boy faltered, not sure.

"We need your help Boy; please!"

Detective Riley put a finger to his lips denoting silence. Timidly the lad came across.

"I didn't do anything wrong, I was just watching the planes."
The boy said, fear in his eyes.

"Relax Lad. We are on a stake-out and we need your help."

"M- me?"

"Yes Boy, what is your name?"

"Brendon Sir. Brendon Miles."

"Well I am Detective Riley and this other man is Detective Dean. We do not want anybody to know we are here – this is special work – have you noticed a seaplane about this airstrip lately?"
Brendon, wide eyed, replied.

"No Sir, but I don't come here often. I have never seen a real seaplane before. I thought you would only see them on the sea!"

"We need to know if there is one hidden in those hangars over there and we can't take the risk of being seen. We want you to ride over and have a look for us." Detective Riley asked, earnestly.

"But, I do not think I would be allowed. I think it is out of bounds for kids; I will get into trouble!" Brendon was afraid.

"Look Brendon, this is police work. You can't get into trouble if we send you but do not let anyone know we sent you; if you do happen to get caught. Just say you did not know and you wanted to have a look inside. Come on Brendon, be a good kid and help us out, you will get a special certificate if no one knows about us!"

"Truly?"

"Truly, no one must know it's police work; okay?"
Brendon lifted his bike over the fence and cycled towards the hangars. From their cover, the two detectives saw Brendon look in the first two hangars unmolested. At the third one, a mechanic caught him snooping around. He was seen to be accosted and sent packing. Brendon high-tailed it back to the fence where he quickly placed his bicycle over and followed it. He hurried to the shrubbery where the detectives awaited him.

"I got caught!" He stated.

"Did you mention us?" Detective Dean asked.

"No Sir. The mechanic just pushed me away and told me the hangars were out of bounds. I came straight back."

"Well?" Detective Riley asked. "Did you see a seaplane?"

"No Sir. The first hangar was empty and the second one has a Tiger Moth in it. The third one I didn't get a good look at but I did not see anything that looked like a floating arrangement. There was a sort of aeroplane Sir, but it was in pieces!"

"Ah, good Lad Brendon. Give me your address and I will see to it that you get a special commendation for helping us. Now promise that you won't go bragging about this at school!"

"No Sir and thanks!" Brendon rode off having supplied the details needed.

Jason was unimpressed when his agents reported back.

"No sign of a seaplane!" He mumbled. "May not be the right airstrip?" Graeme suggested.

"No, that is the one that Ray reckons he and the family were at when they saw one. If it is not in the hangars then they may be only using the strip as a drop-off point. It is probably not where the 'plane is usually housed. I guess we will have to rely on Jim to tell us when he intercepts the next call from Dermutt to Joe. We will just have to wait and see!" Jason turned to Graeme. "Get Riley and Dean to take over from Fox and Carruthers. We might yet be able to 'tail' Joe to an interesting appointment!"

"Something is sure to happen soon." His assistant said, as he went about the arrangements.

It was two days later that Detective Riley asked to urgently see Jason.

"Well, what is so urgent, Max?" He was asked when he entered the Lieutenant's office.

"That trip to the country airstrip has paid off – the kid we had look in the hangars – he just rang me. I knew leaving my business card was a good idea!"

"Well, get on with it – what is so good about it?" Jason was impatient.

"The young lad said that he just saw an aeroplane with pontoons landing at the strip. I daresay by the time we have it covered the thing will have flown the coop though!" Detective Riley had the details written down. He handed the paper to his superior.

"Ahhh good work!" Jason applauded. "So we definitely have the right airstrip, now we only have to get the delivery time right and we can swoop!"

"Be better to let Ratt go with the goods and follow him, before we impound the aircraft; don't you think?" Graeme offered. "The only difficulty with that is, the 'plane could be winging away before Joe leaves!" Jason worried.

Drew Slimmery and Dermutt Schloss were talking over a sore point.

"But if it was at the picnic grounds, well, anybody can use them." Dermutt said, trying to diffuse the situation. "The mechanic was so sure."

Drew thumped the desk, and then went on.

"It was just by co-incidence that our man noticed them. They were too clean-cut he said – 'I can smell a copper anywhere, they're easy to pick'. It was as he was going to get some cigarettes that he noticed them leaving."

Dermutt rested his chin on his fist, cogitating.

"But that does not mean they were there spying. Maybe it was their day off and they went for a break!"

"For crying out loud, be realistic. They would have their wives with them. We cannot afford to take risks. Have the next delivery done at night. I will radio the Captain that the pick-up will be made well out to sea; I only hope the sea is calm. I will let you know when. It will mean that Hewie will have to get the stuff a bit further out, but for the price we are paying, he can manage!"

"How are the 'reefers' going; are the kids interested?" Drew asked after a lapse.

"Yeah! We have a going concern there. So far it has been clean; Charlie and Bernie have the market growing." Dermutt also raised the Pizza question. "I reckon the coast is clear now, we should start pushing it from the new business; what do you say?"

Drew considered this option.

"No – give it a couple of weeks more just to be on the safe side. Have you got those warehouse boys doing anything?" He bored into his underling's eyes.

Dermutt became uneasy.

"Er – no, I er – I thought it better to ease them off. I just give them a bit to keep them on our side. You never know, we may need them again one day!"

He eyed Drew apprehensively and was shocked that Drew agreed with him.

"Yes, good thinking. With Hewie doing such a good job we do not really need them as you say, still, it won't do any harm to keep them there just in case. How is Luntz going at the betting shop?"

"Not so good. There was an undercover bloke nosing about so he had to ease off a bit. I think it will blow over; they only wanted to know what he was doing. They think he is a gambler I reckon." Dermutt was worried that his boss would fly off the handle. He need not have worried.

"Fair enough!" Drew smiled.

Dermutt left with a puzzled expression on his face.

"Stuffed if I can work him out. One minute he is trying to blow my head off, the next he is all co-operative and chummy. Struth, I'll have to be careful with him."

Fatty Burns was disgruntled. He was having a coffee with his co-worker just before retiring for the night and was airing his grievances.

"That blanky Dermutt promised that even if the business was going downhill, the other stuff would more than compensate. Well I have yet to see his promise come true. He said not to contact him – he would contact me – but when? Business is easing off; I could do with a boost!"

"Yair!" The worker agreed. He was a good 'yes man'.

"Sure, the cops did cover the joint when we first opened but that was weeks ago. I could do with a bit of help, the place is going downhill!"

"Yair!" Was the obligatory response.

Fatty looked at him. A cheery grin was all the satisfaction he got.

"Dammit! I'm going to call on him tomorrow and have it out with him. I can't go on like this!"

"Yair!" Fatty again looked at his co-worker and rose for bed.

"Gawd. See you tomorrow." He retired.

Because Fatty never opened the Pizza shop until after lunch, as his business was more for the night timers; he used the morning to call on Dermutt. At eleven in the morning he was at Dermutt's place determined to get the promised 'under-the-counter' assistance needed.

"What the blazes are you doing coming here, get in quick!" Dermutt angrily ordered.

"The business could do with a boost. What about those 'hits' you promised; I really need the extra income?" Fatty worried.

"I said I would call on you and arrange that!" Dermutt was incensed.

"I can't wait forever, I need it now." Fatty heatedly retorted.

"Okay, okay. I had best get the 'all clear' from the big guy though. Give me a couple of days!" Fatty began to cool off.

"It better not be too long or I'm heading back interstate. I left a good business up there to help you out and you left me for dead!"

"Yeah. I know. But we had to ease off because the 'Feds' collared the first shipment. We have that sorted out now and the heats off. You'll get your share soon, just let me get it organized!" Dermutt confided. Fatty left, a little happier than when he came.

Dermutt once more fronted his superior.

"It is a bit sooner than I wanted but we are going to lose Fatty if we don't get some 'stuff' to him and mighty quick. He is threatening to go back interstate!" The underling grovelled. Drew peered at the man with slitted eyes.

"I don't like being told how to do my dealings. He can go back interstate for all that I care."

"But Boss, we went to a lot of trouble to get him here; do you think it wise to upset the man. He is the top pusher you know?" Dermutt dared.

Drew glared back at his adviser.

"Ah. I suppose you are right. See if you can get Silas to make Fatty's stock ready for next week!"

"Gee. Thanks Boss. That should make him happy and get our new outlet viable. I will get on to it right away!" Dermutt grinned.

"Larry popped in the other day." Drew threw at him as Dermutt got up to go.

"Eh. The opposition. What for?" Dermutt was surprised.

His tall skinny superior gave a slimy smile.

"He accused me of 'pinching' one of his men; Hewie."

"I never knew he was in Larry's mob!" Dermutt uttered, bewildered.

"Evidently he was. Never mind, I cleared it up with Larry. Gave him a bit of 'snort', sort of a pacifier if you will, he seemed happy to share him if we give him a 'hand out' occasionally."

"Does that mean there will not be any bloodshed?" Dermutt queried.

"Bloodshed. What bloodshed, Larry and I get on okay; we are friends."

Drew gave a sickly smile. Dermutt looked at Drew, a little as a cat would stare at a mouse it had cornered.

"Friends? Yes, I don't think!" The stubby little man dared.

"Well. That's the way it is, see that you do not cross Hewie; we rely heavily on him. Dismissed."

Once more Dermutt was dismissed. Dark thoughts again entered his head about this domineering lanky boss of his.

CHAPTER EIGHT

Joe was impatiently waiting at the country airstrip for the seaplane. He had already been there an hour and his contact was way overdue. The mechanic sauntered over to him and struck up a conversation.

"Maybe he ditched in the sea!" The man in the dirty overalls opined.

"Nah. Hewie is too good a pilot to let that happen. Probably just a rough sea is keeping him!" Joe determined.

"Yeah. Dunno how them little planes 'ud go if the swell is a bit iffy!" The mechanic frowned.

"I am going to wait another half an hour – if he ain't here by then I will have to go – something must have happened."

"Mind you, he might be no good at night flying, especially with those there pontoons attached."

"Ah! Here he comes now!" Joe cut in as he spied an aeroplane's lights approaching from afar.

"Yeah. See, you was worried for nothing!" The mechanic went back to his bunk.

As the light plane approached, it did not alter its flight path. Disappointed, Joe watched as it flew past the aerodrome and continued on.

"Damn!" Joe exploded. He waited a further fifteen minutes and returned his vehicle empty. As the van made its exit from the small airstrip, the squad of undercover policemen who had been watching dutifully followed.

"Fox and Carruthers, you had better remain here just in case the seaplane does come late." Lieutenant Ferguson ordered. "We will see to whom Joe reports. I have a feeling that something went wrong."

"Yes Sir!"

The bulk of the special squad discreetly took off after the hapless Joe. They saw the van arrive at his home address where he reported the non-arrival to his immediate superior.

"What do you mean it didn't arrive'?" Dermutt angrily asked.

"It just never turned up. I waited for two hours and the only thing to pass was a light plane that kept going. Maybe the sea was too rough!" Joe whined.

Dermutt just looked at his employee, knowing that the man was not lying.

"There must be some explanation, I'll get the boss to ring though and find out what happened."

"The appointment was just after midnight, that's when he had to meet the cargo ship twenty miles off Cape Levinworth. It would not take more than a half hour to secure the rubber dinghy and hoist the crates aboard. Then a half an hour later he should have been at the airstrip. Even if your man only waited an hour for it, there was plenty of time to get there. Something has happened. I will radio the Captain and see if the pick-up was made!" Drew fumed.

Dermutt waited patiently while radio contact was made; Drew gave a nod of assent as he listened. When the conversation was finished, Drew turned to the plump little man who was waiting with furrowed brow.

"The pick-up was made around twelve-thirty, as arranged."

Drew quietly said, his eyebrows twitching.

"Do you think that Hewie has come down somewhere or other before he got to the strip?" Dermutt ventured.

"If he has, he had better contact me soon. If I loose this lot it will just about bust me. There are automatic ouzi's and other assault weapons that will cost me a mint if I lose them; to say nothing of the blocks of hard stuff!" Drew was looking haggard. "By the living dead; Hewie better not cross me!"

Dermutt thanked his lucky stars that he was not the recipient of his boss's ill will.

"Well, what did Jim have to report?"

Jason asked of Graeme when the man came in to the office.

"Yes, I just finished talking with him. You were right; Dermutt went straight to Slimmery and reported that the latest shipment has gone astray. Trailing Schloss was a brilliant business. Jim has the wagon inconspicuously disguised as a workman's quarters in a laneway. The sound is perfect. Slimmery says that the missing shipment is ouzi's and assault weapons as well as a shipment of 'crack'; he reckons it may cost him dearly if he loses this lot!" Graeme smiled.

"It is only money so far as Slimy is concerned. We have to find it before this lot hits the streets!" Jason gravely pondered. "Dermutt was explaining to Slimy that the goods were picked up at the rendezvous point by this 'Hewie', but Hewie did not arrive at the airstrip. Now there is something dicky going on there!"

Graeme looked keenly to his superior. Jason sat back in his chair, thinking.

"One tends to think that Hewie may have had some sort of trouble since he never arrived with the stuff; but with the big brass so worried about it, I wonder?"

"Do you think that he has done a bunk with the goods?" Graeme asked.

"If he has, then I would not like to be in his shoes!" Jason grimly stated.

"Hewie would not have any means of preparing the drugs for the market. He would have had to be more interested in the artillery. Unless he has ideas of selling to another cartel!" Graeme mused.

Jason was a little sceptical.

"I do not think Hewie would double-cross an employer. There must be some other explanation of why he missed the drop. Still nothing from Fox and Carruthers?"

"Not as yet. It must be boring just waiting for someone who does not turn up!" Graeme shook his head.

"Well, it is most important that we find this lot of contraband; put out a bulletin for all uniformed men to be on the look-out for the sea-plane. It will have to land somewhere sometime. Have all airports and especially small airstrips covered, this is a matter of some importance. We must find this shipment!" Jason was most adamant.

Bert Luntz had barely stuffed a heap of banknotes into his pocket, when two detectives swooped upon him and his victim. The white-faced teenager gave little resistance but Bert desperately tried to evade capture. He broke free and made a desperate bid for freedom, throwing packets of powder and reefers into the bushes that he passed. The teenager was handcuffed to a steel picket fence as the detective hastened to assist his partner in pursuit. Bert was apprehended just fifty metres along the way. The evidence gathered as the two returned with their quarry.

"What were you doing Bert; selling headache powders?" Detective Riley caustically quipped.

"I weren't selling nothin'!" Bert defended.

"No! Then what are these packets you discarded when we chased you?" Riley asked.

"What packets – I never had no packets? I was just askin' the kid here where the station is!"

He was handcuffed to the fence beside his victim and searched.

"Got a licence for this hand-gun?" Detective Dean queried.

He was given a sour look, but Bert said nothing. The two were bundled into the unmarked police car and taken to the Police Station.

"Luntz was caught red-handed selling to one of the high school boys!" Graeme Carey informed his superior, as he relinquished the telephone.

"What did he have?" The Lieutenant asked.

"Reefers and heroin, also a hand-gun; unlicensed!" Riley obliged.

"And the young fellow?"

"Detective Dean found a couple of 'reefers' and one hit of heroin on the young bloke. I feel sorry for the kid; I think he was pushed into it by his peers. Riley said he has no priors and the lad has admitted to having tried marijuana once. This was his first attempt at the hard stuff. They evidently frightened the life out of him with the arrest. He was issued with a warrant – being the first time and no record, I think he will be given a warning. Bert is not so lucky, what with the hard stuff, the unlicensed hand gun and resisting arrest to say nothing of selling to minors; he was held in custody!"

"Well that is one pusher off the streets for a while but he is only a piker. We have to nail the big guys!" Jason said with feeling.

"Have Ray ring Dermutt and say he is looking for more cash, just a nibble like that may pay dividends."

"Gee. That is a bit risky don't you think?" Graeme questioned the wisdom of the move.

"We have to locate that missing shipment. He just may get Dermutt to let something slip!" Jason said with feeling.

"Okay but I don't like it; these are only amateurs you know." Graeme worried.

"We have to risk it; they can look after themselves all right. I think the two would have made fine constables; we can only try!"

"Ah well, you are the boss, I just hope your confidence in their ability is well founded." He made the necessary 'phone call.

Ray dutifully did as he was asked by Graeme on Jason's orders.

"It is a bit quiet, I mean no shipments or anything – er – are you sure there is nothing for us? We were getting to like the extra we were earning. This mundane nine-to-five has got whiskers on it; we like to be active!"

"Yeah. Look I'm sorry about that. My boss wants to ease off the warehouse for a bit. You are getting a little extra and you are not doing anything for it; just bide your time for a bit, it'll come!" Dermutt pacified.

"Then you will give us a hoy when something is doing?" Ray eagerly asked.

"Sure thing, I will be in touch; it's just that we are having a little stuff-up at the moment. Nothing for you to get your whiskers in a knot over. Play it cool!" Dermutt tried to sound off-hand. Inwardly he was seething at not hearing from 'Hewie'.

Hewie landed his seaplane at an abandoned farm paddock. He was guided in to the safe landing area by twin rows of half a dozen torches pointed skywards. It was a hairy landing on an unknown field but he had been assured that the strip was safe and flat. His only worry was that he could not see clearly the makeshift wind-sock that had been hastily erected for him. His night flying skills learned as a helicopter pilot in a foreign war-zone, gave him the necessary grounding needed. Hewie was virtually flying blind but his skills were adequate. He landed his aircraft safely. Upon stepping out of his machine, he was dealt a heavy blow on the back of the head. While he lay unconscious, his clothing was torn and dirt was rubbed all over him. He was bound and gagged then placed into his aircraft and left to be found. His assailants dispersed taking his cargo with them.

"Senior Detective Ron Shell of the local C.I.D. on the line Sir"

Jim Linton, the Intelligence telephone operator told Graeme Carey.

"Yes Jim, what is it?"

"There is talk of your mob wanting to locate a seaplane?"

"That is right. Have you got something?" Graeme asked with interest.

"Yes, up on the high flats near Warrendale the local boys have found one with the pilot trussed up. They say he has been rough-housed and they are waiting for instructions."

"Oh good, give me the details and I shall get some people up there right away!"

The details were given. Graeme and Jason sped off hastily to the abandoned farm.

"What is Hewie doing landing his plane on an abandoned farm?" Graeme asked of Jason as they drove along.

"It has me beat. Unless he had mechanical trouble."

"I do not think that mechanical trouble would get him bashed up. "Graeme offered.

"No. And I am willing to bet that the cargo has been nicked too!" Jason observed.

"The dogs will be along soon. I organized that like you asked." Graeme spoke as he scratched his head. "I take it that you do not think that there will be anything in the plane, so the dogs are just to find out if there have been any drugs involved?"

"Bingo, give that man a cigar!" Jason smiled.

Dawn was breaking as the two officers arrived. There was a police van at the scene and the pilot was handcuffed in it. Two uniformed men stood up and saluted when they saw their superior officers.

"We have the man secured as you suggested Sir!" The most senior of the two uniformed men said. Jason nodded and asked.

"What does he have to say for himself?"

"Just that he had to make an emergency landing in the dark and when he alighted, he was mobbed. That is all, Sir."

"Now Hewie, what is the real story?" Jason addressed the incensed pilot.

"Ay. How come you know my name – I ain't never met you?"

"We checked the registration details in case you pinched the aircraft. It is far from the sea!"

"Oh. Yeah!"

"Now, what is your story?" Jason urged.

"Like I told the coppers. I had to make an emergency landing and when I did, some stinkin' hounds mugged me. There weren't nuthin' aboard for them to pinch so they mugged me outa spite I reckon!"

The dog squad came and interrupted the conversation. Jason locked the van door and went to them.

"Ay! Lemme out, I ain't done nuthin', I was a victim!" Hewie bawled, all to no avail.

After the dogs had free rein over the cargo bay, the dog squad reported their findings and left. Jason returned to Hewie and told him the bad news.

"We have reason to believe that the aircraft has recently been carrying contraband. You will be taken to the Station for further questioning!"

That was it. The aeroplane was left and they departed accept for one of the uniformed men, who had the unenviable job of securing the area as a suspected crime scene. With repeated questioning, Hewie stuck to his story. He had been out on a pleasure trip and when he returned on his way to a mate's place; he had mechanical trouble and ditched where he could. In the dark that was the best he could do and as soon as he got out to see what the cause of his trouble was; a mob of blokes were all over him. They roughed him up and tied him. That is all he knew about it. He did not know what was in previous cargoes he has carried, he just delivered them. After twenty four hours, Jason could hold him no longer on the sniff of dogs' evidence. As there was no hard evidence; Hewie was set free until a magistrate decided what his case was.

"Where the hell have you been?" Dermutt angrily burst out when Hewie rang.

"Some thieving double-crosser from the ship held me at gunpoint and made me fly to some outlandish country farm. When I landed the plane there, they rolled me and left me for dead. I was bound and would have died in that isolated place, except that the coppers found me and then they arrested me. You'll have to get me a lawyer; I gotta go to court!"

"Bloody hell! You are costing us a mint. I will have to let the big bloke know. Are our goods still in the plane?" Dermutt cursed.

"I dunno – no the dog squad has been through it and the damned animals sniffed the stuff, but the coppers couldn't pin nuthin' on me – so I s'pose the lot has been took. I woke up in the divvy van!"

Silence greeted this last remark. Dermutt was thinking.

"Yes, we'll have your case covered. I had best get instructions off the boss. Stay at the hotel where we can get in touch with you!" Dermutt hung up the phone.

"Hi-jacked. All of it?"

Drew thought about pulling his revolver on the hapless Dermutt, and then remembering the last time he did that; changed his mind. Dermutt only fired one shot and knocked the pistol out of his hand. Seething, he began to resemble the snake his cohorts likened him to; a slithering slimy predator.

"What the blazes is going on with these shipments? First we had a leak and got rid of old Johnson. Then the warehouse stuff got seized and we found it linked to the

Richmond cutting room – now our foolproof import pick-up gets hi-jacked. By the living dead someone is going to pay for this!"

He waved Dermutt away to do some high class thinking. As he left the premises, Dermutt had grave thoughts about his boss. 'I'll have to get in first; the bugger is going to pull a gun on me soon. He damn near did then, it isn't my fault but I get blamed for it. I will have to do him; he is getting to be very unstable lately. Too much merchandise is going astray lately. I don't trust that Hewie – something stinks there!'

"So! Slimmery is getting desperate at all these losses, Dermutt is running around like a March hare and Hewie still claims he is the innocent victim; yet he tells Dermutt the goods were hi-jacked. That is different to the line he gave us – 'I was running empty', he said. So who were the hi-jackers?" Jason mused.

"That tape will have to be kept for the case when it comes up; it is vital evidence." Graeme stated the obvious.

"Yes, but you know these magistrates -" Jason made the point "- they do not place much credence in tapes, that can be easily manipulated."

"What are your thoughts on these 'hi-jackers'?" Graeme wanted to know.

"Yes, now that is the conundrum. It would not be one of the ships crew; Hewie reckons there were a mob of them. Maybe one of the crew was responsible for holding Hewie up, but he would have to have backup at the country farm. Hewie said when he got out of the plane he was ambushed. Why didn't the attacker ambush him in the plane when it stopped? Then the goods had to be man-handled out of the plane and into the get-away vehicle; that would take at least one other person!"

"If you ask me, I think Hewie made the story up. I reckon he flew solo to this farm and his mate has double-crossed him!" Graeme suggested.

"I am beginning to agree with you, the trouble is – Hewie got pretty roughed up – one would not think that was deliberate." Jason said with a frown.

He drummed his fingers on the desk, a sure sign that he was worried.

"That seems to negate the fact of Hewie working together with these hi-jackers, but if he flew solo to the farm; why would he do it. Unless his mates turned against him!" Graeme was sceptical.

"The main point here is we still do not know where the contraband has got to; that is the main worry!" Jason thumped his fist into his other hand.

"There are no tyre tracks on the grass either, so we can't even be sure what type of vehicle was involved." The Sergeant murmured.

"I had better have another talk with this here 'Hewie', you never know; he just might let something slip." Jason got up to go just as Detective Lynton approached to knock on his door.

"Oh, I am glad I caught you." He said. "I intercepted a call between Drew Slimmery and an underworld contact of his – er – name of Stroud, 'hit man Stroud', he is known as; - er – comes from interstate!"

"And?" Jason asked.

"It appears that Drew has been fleeced so much that he is getting desperate. He wants this bloke to join Larry Crumpers mob, sort of on the quiet, and see if Larry had anything to do with his missing contraband!"

"So! We have trouble with the opposition. Now that is a new stance. The opposition is now involved; that may explain the mugging of Hewie. Good work Jim!"

Jason was now armed with something new that he could hit Hewie with; he hastened to see what this new line would lead to.

Chapter Nine

Hewie furtively looked carefully before leaving the hotel. The time was past nine in the evening as the pilot made his way with meticulous care, to a taxi-cab rank. He arrived in one of the near-city northern suburbs at a rather seedy looking gymnasium, where he was allowed into the inner sanctum by a bruiser of a man, after having given the pass-word and stated his business. He was frisked to see he had no hidden weapons before being let in to an office. It was marked 'manager'. A man who had the appearance of a boxer, as his nose was spread across his face and he had enormous arms and physique; arose to leave as Hewie entered.

" – and remember to take a dive in the fifth round!"

Larry said as the man passed Hewie in the doorway.

"Ah, the unfortunate man who got 'mugged' and lost all his merchandise!" Larry smiled hugely at his accomplice. "Hope the boys did not rough you up too much – it is going to pay you well, just the same."

"Yeah! It went over real well. Fooled everyone, Slimy, the cops and even that dopey captain. I gotta hand it to ya Boss; that was a brainwave. To top it all off, Slimmery is copping the legal bills." Larry grinned at Hewie.

"Oh boy. That I like even more. I knew when I spoke to him that I'd find a way to get even with him for being so bloody high and mighty. All this 'I am better than thou' business makes me sick. He is no better than an ordinary dead-beat. The way he chucks a chest at me gives a bloke the irrits. Now, do you think we can pull it off again with the next shipment?"

"Aw, I don't think that is a good idea Boss. He could get suspicious, how about we let the next one go through and take the following one; that way they won't get me in the gun. Besides, it will be better if we wait for a big one!"

Hewie raised his eyebrows in query to see how his boss reacted. Larry frowned at the audacity of his hireling, and then nodded absently to himself.

"Okay, you could be right. Yeah; come to think of it you are!" He went to a hidden safe in a cupboard which was built-in. Returning with a large wad of notes.

"Wow!" Hewie could not help himself saying. "Now that is worth getting roughed up over!"

"Yeah, an' there's more where that came from, so be sure you watch out and don't do anything foolish – like splash your dough around!"

"No, I won't boss!"

When Hewie had gone, Larry feeling rather pleased with himself, made his way to the gymnasium where his boxers were preparing for their next bouts. He was waved across to where his head trainer was in urgent conversation with a stranger. There were two very large bruisers surrounding the man.

"What is the trouble?" Larry asked the head trainer.

"This 'ere coot – reckons his name is Stroud an' 'e wants to talk wiv the boss!"

"Yeah. What do you want with the boss?" Larry asked, sizing the stranger up.

"I just hit town from interstate, they say I should see the boss of this here place for a job. Are you the Boss?"

"What sort of job?"

"I can get rid of undesirables – I'm a bodyguard!"

"Yeah? Prove it. These two are annoying me."

Larry motioned towards the two bruisers. Quick as a flash Hector Stroud had a pistol aimed at the two and motioned for them to get away. With cries of 'shit' the very large men backed off.

"Okay – okay, I believe you. Put that thing away!" Larry said in urgent haste.

Then as his head trainer excused.

"We wos tryin' to frisk ím when ya come in but 'e said 'e'd blow our 'eads orf!"

"All right Stroud, come with me!" Larry took the man back to his office.

Back at S.I.O. headquarters, Graeme interrupted Jason again.

"Looks like we may have found the missing guns!"

"Oh! How so?" Jason looked up from his paperwork.

"Just got a report in about a group of radicals playing war games up in the mountains two hundred kilometres from town. The locals are complaining of the distant noise of firearms. From the reports it appears that ouzi's or some such weapons are being used." Graeme said as he slapped the notes he took on to Jason's desk.

"What have the local boys to say about it?"

"They are making an effort now – they just thought we should know in case of slip-ups. These radical groups are very hard to pin-point; time the locals get there, they have gone underground. It is a part of their training I'm told."

"Yes, it sounds like we should send up a scouting squad. Send a wire that the locals are not to make too big a presence there until we have had a chance to properly assess the situation. If we can find out where they got the guns, we could be led to the source!"

When a contingent of agents did arrive at the mountain retreat, there were no radicals much less the hardware they were thought to be using; to be seen. A fairly thorough search of the area was conducted and though signs of a war-zone were apparent, nothing of concrete evidence was happened upon; until one officer noticed a broken branch. Having notified his senior of the fact, a more minute examination of the near vicinity was made. They found quite a few bullets embedded in some trees. With meticulous care they were recovered and taken to the forensic branch. The slugs and many bullet casings found were proven to be the same as those that would be used in the automatic ouzi assault rifles. A trap was set with two undercover officers dressed in attire for game shooting; they were to remain in the vicinity until the radicals were next in training. The duty sergeant was double-checking his notes.

"There does not seem to be anything that we can do about it at the moment, so I suppose you can pick up your aircraft. Your papers, licence the craft itself are all in order but we will be keeping an eye out for any illegal cargo you may be carrying. We catch you with anything illicit – and bingo – we will confiscate the aeroplane. Think yourself lucky that the dog squad only had a smell to go on; nothing of actual proof."

Begrudgingly, the officer gave Hewie the 'all clear' and he was allowed to re-claim ownership of his aircraft.

Dermutt Schloss was once more in the office of Drew Slimmery; their discussion was regarding the loss of so many shipments in such a short period.

"There must still be a leak – or leaks – in the network." Drew worried.

"So far your lot are clear, my contacts are covered but I have my doubts regarding this 'Hewie'. I do not know about his story of being 'skyjacked' by one of the ships crew. There is something fishy there. I have got a new man in Larry's employ; he is a real hard case, so if Larry is involved we will soon know. That story of Hewie being mugged at the farm – I don't know – he was certainly roughed up, but was he roughed up by some outside mob who belonged to the ship; or was it by some other concern?"

Drew heaved a sigh of frustration.

"What about Larry? He could have a hand in it!" Dermutt suggested.

Drew looked at him, then slowly shook his head.

"Nah! Larry is too dense for that sort of caper. He is more into the 'stand over' tactics; he only knows thuggery and fight-fixing. Nah, he's too dense, that is why I put my man in there though; just in case." Drew thoughtfully mused.

"Well Hewie could not have pulled it off on his own, he had to have help. He was bound and gagged and woke up in the divvy wagon. Someone took the guns and drugs out of his plane." Dermutt stated with feeling.

"Yes!" Drew cogitated. "But whom?"

"Do you think Hewie set it up so that he and his mates could make a 'killing'? I wouldn't put it past him!" Dermutt gave his boss a severe look.

"Hewie knows better than to double-cross me, he knows that Stroud would be set on to him. I told Hewie when I first hired him that if he crosses me, he gets a delivery that may blow him out of the air. He has been warned. No, I trust Hewie; it's his mates I do not have much confidence in!" Drew quietly nodded to himself, his mind in turmoil. "I really think that Hewie may have been outwitted by someone he trusted. It may very well be one of the ship's crew. He said that was when he made the pick-up that he got hi-jacked. That sounds like it was a crew member, someone who was in the know!"

"What about Fatty. Are we going to get him started this week?" Dermutt waited while Drew thought about this last question.

"Haven't got much stock since we have been losing so much; can he hang about for a bit do you think?" The question was a probe; most unusual for his boss to even ask.

"I will have a talk with him; I should be able to keep him interested if the promise is kept for next week. He is getting impatient but I will kid him along."

Dermutt seemed sure of himself and his powers of persuasion.

"Right! Now we will only push a small shipment through this time. Get Hewie to pick it up and we will keep a close eye on him. Better see if Charlie will go with him as a little insurance in case any one is thinking to hi-jack the shipment this time!" Drew cunningly smiled.

"Hey; that is a brilliant idea!" Dermutt exclaimed. Drew smiled at the praise.

Charlie Orso and Hewie duly arrived with the small parcel of dope one quiet evening. The seaplane landed on a little-known paddock on the outskirts of a country town nearest to the outer suburbs of the city. Charlie quit the aeroplane with the parcel, bundled it into the waiting vehicle driven by his partner and both the plane and vehicle departed the scene with haste. Bernie Brocchio smiled smugly as they motored away.

"Looks like that pick-up went easily." He grinned.

"Yeah! Piece of cake!" Charlie admitted.

Dermutt and Fatty were in secret conversation in the back room of a hotel.

"Now I will get Charlie to make the deliveries when the stuff is processed. He will have a white coat on and will be delivering flour. The reefers and hard stuff will be packed into some ordinary flour packets, so for goodness sakes don't get them mixed. He will come at a different time weekly; we do not want his movements to be monitored. Now I know you know what you are doing but please be careful with new customers for the first couple of weeks. This business is getting to be too well saturated with 'pigs' lately. The boss is expecting you to be professional and not make any mistakes. Once we get your show on the road, well, there is big money in it for us all!"

"She'll be Jake!" Fatty smiled, looking like the fat pig he was.

"Okay. We had best leave separately."

Dermutt returned to his place of abode, his head in turmoil. Things had been moving fairly smoothly up until those two snoopers had interfered with that shipment of guns at Arnold Johnson's place. He tried to 'bump' them off but they had proven smarter than Joe and Bert. Then Drew ordered that as they were in charge at the warehouse where their shipments were processed, perhaps they could be persuaded to 'come over' to their side and push the shipments through. That had worked well but there was a 'leak', somewhere in their organization; it proved to be at the Richmond cutting room. When at first Drew had ordered that Arnold be 'taken' out by Ray and Gerry, as a suspect of the 'leak' although Dermutt did not believe that Arnold was the leak, Ray and Gerry proved that they were up to it; in fact they were very impressive. Just to be sure of them, Drew ordered that 'Doc' Lomax give them a 'truth' drug. Under the influence of that, heavy questioning gave no inkling but that the two were loyal to the underworld cause. Too many of their shipments were being intercepted and tampered with. There was still a 'leak', their cutting rooms at the lower slopes on the outer suburban ranges; was raided and five good men were arrested. Then they tried a different method of importing the goods. Hewie was introduced and the shipments were picked up at sea and delivered inland to a country airstrip. This was successful for awhile but the 'feds' were suspected of monitoring the airstrip and then Hewie got high jacked. 'Come to think of it', he thought. 'The feds may be working independently to get a shipment for themselves; it is possible. No, that is a bit far-etched'. Dermutt scratched his head. Then we brought 'Fatty' Burns from interstate and after the usual check to see that the pizza place was 'clean', he was left alone. Now after he threatened to go back, Fatty was given the okay by Drew to start pushing some 'stuff'. How successful that will be had yet to be seen. Meanwhile, Bert Luntz was picked up selling to minors and put away for a while. 'Serves the dope right for being caught', was the unspoken thought of Dermutt. Then because the inland airstrip was being monitored by the feds, a small shipment of 'hard stuff' was picked up by Charlie Orso and Bernie Brocchio. This one came through all right. Hopefully the leak had been stopped.

Detective Jason Ferguson of the Secret Intelligence Organization made a surprise visit to Ray Cress at his home. Cindy answered the door chimes.

"Yes, how may I help you?" She said with a smile.

Jason took off his hat and offered his card. Cindy looked and then asked.

"What do you want with me?"

"Who is it dear?" Ray peeped from the kitchen. Then exclaimed. "Good grief! Come in Jason."

Cindy stood aside to let the man enter. She closed the door after him, looking expectantly to her husband.

"Cup of coffee?" Ray smiled.

"Thanks, I am sorry to impose on your private life like this but we are at a bit of a difficult time and need outside help."

Cindy busied herself with the preparations as Ray offered a chair for the visitor. Her heart was thumping; this could only mean bad news for her; so she thought. As Cindy placed the crockery for their refreshment, Jason elaborated.

"Slimmery keeps altering the timetable and there is a new player in the game! Er, how are things at home here?" He looked first at Cindy and then at Ray.

"Cindy knows I am working in with you but not much else." Ray said.

"I believe we had best let her know a little more so that there will not be any marital difficulties between you two!"

"If you think that is wise – go for it!" Ray authorised.

Jason looked earnestly in Cindy's direction and almost pleaded to her.

"Ray and Gerry have been helping us with our inquiries into a drug and gun-running cartel. Now as the foremen in charge of the warehouse, they have been most helpful in notifying us of any shipments that come in for the cartel." He paused to see if there was any dissent from Cindy; noting that she was fairly composed, he continued.

"I do not know what Ray has told you but both he and Gerry have been sworn in as Probationary Officers for their own protection, so as they will be covered in case things get out of hand." Cindy looked at Ray as if she already knew but said nothing. "Well now we need the two of them to assist us a little bit further. You see, the cartel also hired Ray and Gerry to aid them in getting their shipments processed through customs a little more easily, however, because of your husband and Gerry, the cartel have now by-passed the customs warehouse and the cartel have made private arrangements to get the stuff into the country." Jason frowned as he tried to phrase the next question. "What we need now is for Ray and Gerry to get a little higher into their confidence, so we can stamp out this menace to our kids and country!"

Cindy looked a little white in the face as she noted.

"But Ray is not trained in police work. It could be dangerous; he could get injured or – killed!" Her fears for the man she loved were starting to show now.

"There is very little danger Sweet, the police have undercover men protecting me at all times; you know that. Don't you remember the man reading a newspaper every morning in the park opposite, and the man sweeping the streets? Jo-Anne had a Special Undercover watching her at school even; do not worry overly on that score we are well protected!" Ray tried to placate his wife; she smiled at him with a worried frown.

"Yes, but I do worry just the same."

Jason eased her feelings a little more with the statement.

"It is not as if they will actually be under fire. Far from it, all we want them to do is keep their eyes and ears open for the slightest clue of what is going on with the cartel; that is all!"

With a rather sickly smile, Cindy shrugged.

"I have a good man and I do not want to lose him!" She pleaded.

Ray rose and gave her a cuddle.

"Do you think I am going to take foolish risks when I have such a champion?"

He kissed her on the lips, passionately.

"Right, so long as you realize that the risks are minimal, although they are still risks, and knowing a little of what your husband is experiencing; you may be less harsh on him when he suddenly has to keep an appointment for us." Jason smiled reassuringly. "We will not expect him to take suicidal risks but some of the things that have to be done, are better left to an outside body so as to avert suspicion. Do you understand that?"

Cindy gave Jason her assurance that she would not unduly stand in the way of Ray doing his bit for society.

"But mind you, if I find you are not looking after his best interests - quick smart I will pull the plug!" She gravely frowned at Jason.

"Fair enough!" He said.

"Right!" Jason changed the subject. "Let us get down to the real business of the evening, the reason why I had to come here!" Cindy arose.

"It is probably better that I do not know, so I will get about finishing the dishes."

She went back to the kitchen. Ray was all attention as Jason got to the nitty-gritty of details and planning that he had in mind for the two would-be detectives.

"The warehouse is no longer being used as a gateway to bring the stuff into the country; therefore you two are redundant so far as Slimy and Dermutt are concerned. Now you have managed to be enlisted into the cartel and have proved your trustworthiness to them. We do not want that advantage to be wasted, so we have to up the ante; see if we can have you take on more of a working part in the cartel. This is the only way to get positive proof that Slimy and Dermutt are working together on the gun-running and drugs."

"And how do you propose we do that?" Ray wanted to know.

"Perhaps if you asked this Dermutt for some way of getting a little bit extra - ?"

"We already tried that, he just fobbed us off!" Ray hastened to explain.

"Yes, I know. So far as Dermutt knows, he thinks you two reckon he deals only in guns. He has not mentioned anything about drugs to you has he?"

Jason firmly grasped his chin with finger and thumb.

"No, I don't think so." Ray pondered, not at all sure about that. "I can not recall any mention of him asking us to push his drugs through, it was just crates of 'merchandise' that he mentioned."

"Right. Now Captain Vaughn has suggested that you try to buy some hard drugs because you can make a 'killing' with them, to a new acquaintance you have just met at the warehouse. Ask Dermutt if he knows where you can 'acquire' them. Say your new buyer is only interested in quality stuff, but, he is prepared to pay for it. We will cover the cost; only make certain you aren't too eager. Do you think you can swing it?"

Jason looked sceptically at Ray, who considered the proposition, then nodded.

"Sure!"

CHAPTER TEN

"Well, what is so urgent that you called me in?" Dermutt demanded.

Ray quietly sipped his coffee while he gathered his thoughts.

"You - er – you don't seem to need Gerry and my services any more and the little bit of money we are getting now is not worth the worry. I just thought I would see if you did not mind if we wriggled out this situation, I mean, you know; there has not been a raid for a while and you have nothing for us to push through." Ray looked worried, and then continued. "I was not sure if your boss would mind if we backed out or not, I mean we are of no use to you!"

His frowning features gave Dermutt to understand that he was genuine in his wish to have the 'mob' off his back. The chubby little man peered long into Ray's face. Then offered.

"Look, I am not sure if we are going to use you again but the boss said it was good business to keep you on as insurance. We do not know what the future holds but we have you here and if you go, well, we will have to start over again." Dermutt thought to himself for a bit, and then made the suggestion. "Tell you what – if we double what we are giving you now – put you almost back to what you were getting; will that keep you on the job?"

Ray forced a smile. Gosh Gerry will probably go crook at me but I reckon that is a good deal – yes – I think that will make him change his mind. Thanks, we will carry on as usual and let you know if and when they raid us again – gee – thanks!" Ray brightened. Dermutt got up to go when as an afterthought, Ray asked.

"Oh. Before you go."

"Yeah, what?" The chubby man turned back to ask.

Ray, with tongue in cheek, and finger over his lips to denote a private conversation; motioned for Dermutt to come closer.

"I have a rather keen enquiry from a business associate of mine who wants to know if I have any connections to heroin or ecstasy. I told him no because I don't, but said I would try and find out. Now I know you only deal in guns – but – I thought maybe you could give me a pointer to who might be a good bloke to try. This business associate has the money and only wants the 'good stuff', whatever that is. He reckons that he is desperate and I had to be careful who I asked. I really don't know anybody but I thought I would ask you if you knew where I could get it for him!"

Dermutt looked Ray deeply in the eyes to see if he was trying to put one over on him. Ray shrugged.

"No, I did not think that was your kettle of fish. Ah well, I can only ask!"

"Tell you what!" Dermutt said. "I do happen to know a bloke that could get me some. What if I managed to 'acquire' what you need and paid you that instead of cash. How would that suit you? Then what you charge him for it, well, that is your business. You may be able to make a bigger profit that way!" Dermutt raised his eyebrows in query, thinking that this suggestion would get him another outlet for his drugs and maybe even a couple of new 'customers', if Ray and Gerry fell into the trap.

"Hey! That is smart thinking!" Ray pretended it was a novel idea.

"Okay, I'll drop some off for you – I will just pop in sometime – all right?"

"Yes, make it soon though!" Ray saw him out. Both had satisfied smiles.

Jason was suitably impressed when Ray reported to him on the quiet. "So from what you tell me he went for it and does not suspect anything?"

The Lieutenant said.

"No, he just thinks I am an opportunist trying to supplement my income."

Ray informed.

"Good, perhaps this may lead us to something like concrete evidence. We have to try and implicate the big two, mind you, I still think there is a higher power behind all of this – maybe even an international connection – time will tell!" Jason held out a hand which Ray took. "Thanks Ray, see if you can wiggle your way into their confidence enough for us to catch the two big noises with their sticky fingers stuck right into the pot!"

"Yes if I play it cool and don't get over eager or over confident, well, one never knows!"

"Er – Jason!"

"Yes. Is there something else?"

"When you called in the other day you mentioned something about a 'new player', what new player?" Ray keenly asked.

"Oh yes. I meant to elaborate on that. Just as well you reminded me. Now I do not know if it will involve you two or not, but it is always advisable to be careful – forewarned and all that. This new player is a hard case who has been brought down from interstate. He is a cunning and shrewd deadly killer. Name of Stroud – hit-man Hec Stroud – do not take him lightly. I have not found out what his function is as yet, but we intercepted a call from Slimmery, he had him brought down for a purpose; just what that purpose is we are not sure of but it has something to do with the missing contraband from the plane. He may be given the task of hounding down the 'leak'; if he crosses your path we want to know immediately. Got that. Immediately!"

Jason stressed the point. Ray, with a grim look, just nodded.

Hector Stroud sat with a smug expression on his – by no means pretty – features. Larry was spelling out in detail just what he expected of his 'new' man.

"Your job is to follow me around like a shadow, especially when I have outside business to attend. I won't have you in my back pocket but just place yourself somewhere behind to watch my back. There is another mob who just may be thinking of 'doing away' with me and I want somebody I can rely on, to keep a watch out for opportunist assassinators. I am pretty sure that the opposition would not mind if I sort of, disappeared." Larry smiled at Hec with a self-important defiant expression that smacked of egotism. "Now my boys are good and they can mix it with anybody in a brawl, but they ain't thinkers. I need a good thinker at my back because I sort of, encourage enemies. In my line of business it is par for the course; you understand?"

"Yep! That's what I'm good at. Don't worry, No one'll see me but I'll be there!"

Stroud said himself an egotist.

"Okay, in the gym here I should be all right, just mingle with the boys and make yourself known to them!"

Stroud swaggered out and did as he was ordered by his new boss. Word had got around that the boss had hired a 'protector' and those who witnessed his introduction, were very wary of him. That 'Hec' Stroud was a person not to be messed with, soon had the gymnasium fraternity eyeing the man off warily.

"Freeze!"

The order was said in an undertone as the two undercover detectives were sleeping in their tent.

"What the --??" The most senior of the two exclaimed.

"Quiet, no noise and do not move."

As the detectives roused and turned to the disturbance, they could discern half a dozen armed soldiers quickly infiltrate and take over the tent.

"Do you know who we are?" The senior man asked.

An ouzi combat rifle was poked to his forehead and he was forced down.

"I don't give a damn who you are, you will do as you are told. That's an order!" The voice behind the weapon snarled.

"Couple of police issue hand pieces Sir, and handcuffs." A soldier said, offering the weapons for inspection.

"So, coppers?" The voice said. "Blindfold and handcuff them, we will have to take them to the Commander, it's up to him what is to be done with them. They are trespassing on a military base. Just as well the Duty Sergeant told us to make sure there were no campers about. If we stared firing they could have been slaughtered!"

The detectives knew that they were in a sticky situation when one of the soldiers could be heard to say, "We might have to slaughter them anyway; this action is supposed to be top secret!"

It was mid afternoon of the next day, when the two detectives were able to report to Jason.

"We spent the night in an army tent cuffed and bound with our heads covered, then still covered in the morning we were taken to a remote part of the bush and left to fend for ourselves. We managed to wriggle out of the blindfolds and the ropes but could not get the cuffs off. After hearing passing vehicles we made it to a road and managed to flag down a truckie. We had a job trying to convince him we were detectives with the cuffs on, perseverance paid off and he eventually got us to the local station. It was not very pleasant; the local boys had a great laugh at our expense. We took the local boys up to the camp but the place was deserted. I know they used it that night because we heard them. There was not the faintest trace of them or that they had been there the next day. Vanished completely; I doubt that they will return now that we know of their activities!" Detective Colin Rhumps dejectedly reported into the telephone.

"Did you or detective McCritchley see a face?" Jason asked.

"Evan didn't, he was face down when they held us at gun point. I had a gun pressing on my forehead but only got a fleeting glimpse in the dark Sir. He was a young man with a square sort of face, but that is all I can tell you Sir!"

"Well, when you get back, report to me. We may be able to get some sort of a fix on that one!"

"Yes Sir! Oh. We recovered our sedan; it was where we left it. Evidently the rebels never touched it because we went over the thing with a fine toothed comb and there were no finger prints or any other interference with it, Sir!"

"No, I would not have expected them to go near your car when they found you were detectives. They want to remain incognito, the less known about them the better it is for them. Right; I will see you when you get back!" Jason hung up and sat thinking.

"I am on my way to pick up a big one now Boss!" Hewie said into the telephone.

"Good! Now just like we planned the other day. Use the same country farm strip, you know, that one that used to be used when you was a crop-duster; we ain't gonna rough you up this time. I'll have the boys just tie and blindfold you, a whisper will get through to Slimy that your plane is down and you are in trouble. We won't use that strip again. I'll have to let Slimy know before the cops get on to it, we don't want them interfering again!" Larry gave a satisfied smirk as he replaced the telephone. Hewie set about flying his seaplane out to the ship just off the coast at a prearranged rendezvous.

Meanwhile back at the office used by Drew Slimmery; he was in urgent conversation with Dermutt.

"Now Charlie and Bernie are working with Hewie, the shipments should be a lot safer. They are both pretty dense but they will do the job okay!"

"Yes I hope so, we can not afford to lose this one; it is a lot larger than anything previous we brought in. The small shipment we used as a decoy got through fine, so I suppose this one should." Dermutt agreed.

"Now you did tell Hewie to come down in the same place as he did for the little one?" Drew double checked.

"Yes, and because of the importance of this one, I also have Joe giving them a hand. He will be waiting with Bernie at the landing spot." Dermutt gave a satisfied smile.

"Good thinking." Drew arose and walked up and down his office; nervously. "This is a most important lot for us. We are drying out with the damned coppers raiding us and now someone outside the cartel filching one shipment. It was a big one too, hell when I find out who is responsible for it, they'll finish up at the bottom of the river with concrete boots!" His demeanour spelled rough justice for the one responsible.

The time had passed three in the morning when Bernie Brocchio reported to Dermutt.

"The seaplane never turned up. No sign of Charlie or Hewie!"

"What?" Dermutt dropped the coffee he had just made to keep him awake. "Not again. Don't tell me it's been snatched again!"

"I dunno Boss. We waited for two hours and there was no sign of the thing. Maybe there has been a mix-up on the landing site; Hewie might have gone to another strip!" Bernie hoped.

"Hell! Slimy will blow his top. Get back in case he's been delayed. We will give him until daylight; hurry!"

Bernie sped off in pursuit of his immediate boss's directive. 'He won't show I reckon the cargo had been filched again!' He thought to himself.

Joe Ratt just nodded, he was almost asleep. Daylight was well and truly set in when the worried pair turned up again at the residence of Dermutt Schloss.

"Nothing Boss, the only things that were flying was the magpies; all quiet, nothing else moved." Bernie shrugged.

Dermutt just glared at the two as they stood wondering whether he would explode or not. Dermutt just told them to get some sleep; he now had the unenviable job of informing his superior. Remembering that Drew was liable to have a short fuse; Dermutt deemed it better to ring him instead of risking a confrontation which could mean

Drew's gun could go off before Dermutt got out of the way; he took the risk of the Feds overhearing and rang.

As Hewie and Charlie were winging back after having picked up the contraband from the ship, and before they approached the shoreline; Hewie put a pistol to Charlie's head and fired. The man died immediately. He was unceremoniously dumped out of the plane to disappear in the darkness to a watery grave. Hewie rued the fact of having to put a hole in the fuselage of his beloved aircraft but it was a necessity. He would patch it and clean up the bloodstains before reporting to Dermutt. Upon landing, the goods were removed efficiently and as pre-arranged, Hewie was bound and gagged; then left in his aeroplane.

An anonymous caller rang Drew Slimmery and reported the aircraft abandoned, and then hung up.

"Hey! Who is this – hello, hello – bugger you; answer me damn you!"

Drew was fuming when Dermutt called a few minutes later.

"Just got an anonymous call – the shipment has been grabbed again hasn't it?"

Drew snarled into the handset.

"Ay? Yes, but how did you know so soon?" Dermutt was nonplussed.

"The smart arsed buggers got to the 'phone and told me where the 'plane is, geez some heads are going to roll!"

Dermutt thanked the 'powers that be' he had the foresight to ring instead of fronting the boss in person.

Bernie and Joe were ordered to see what was left of the seaplane and its cargo; if any. They found Hewie bound and gagged on the floor of his aircraft. When he was untied his first words were:-

"Hell. Again, I got rolled again. Dermutt's line must be bugged, how else would they know I was flying last night?"

"The stuff all gone?" Joe looked about the cargo hold. Bernie asked.

"Where's Charlie?"

"Huh? Ain't he here? That must be the shot I heard!" Hewie looked bewildered.

"How come they shot Charlie and not you?" Bernie persisted.

"I heard them take him outside – then there was a scuffle – he must have resisted them!"

"Charlie was my mate. He better not have been shot; I'm gunna revenge him!" Bernie promised.

"Yeah, I'll help you too – it could have been me!" Hewie snarled with venom.

"Well, we better get back and report to Dermutt." Joe growled. He knew the pickings would be minimal now that another lot of goods were lost.

"Hewie is going to come in when he gets back from the airport. The plane was empty and Hewie was all trussed and gagged. He reckons he heard a shot. There certainly was no sign of Charlie about. Hewie reckons he must have resisted them so they shot him, but we didn't find no body. What would the blokes wot pinched the stuff want with his body?" Bernie grizzled.

Dermutt looked deeply at his henchmen.

"Something stinks here. Unless Charlie is in with them; he could be the 'leak'!"

The plump little man stroked his chin in anguish.

"Nah! Charlie was true to our cause, he wouldn't do nuthin' like that. I am going to find out what happened to him and if he was shot by these buggers; look out!" Bernie vowed.

"Yes, I do not take kindly to my men being butchered either." Dermutt quietly said. "I will not see the big fellow until Hewie reports to me – the head can hear his story first-hand."

Chapter Eleven

Hewie smiled expansively when he slipped into Larry's office.

"Must have been a good haul, Slimmery is furious by all accounts, according to Dermutt, anyhow!" Hewie was in high spirits. "Of course I was lambasted by the fat little prick; he reckons it was my fault that the goods were hi-jacked. I stood up to him I did, told him there was probably a leak on his side and he could stick his mouldy job. I said I was not going to get roughed up and then told it was my fault. He ended up apologising and said not to get my bowyangs warped just yet. He said he was just letting off steam!" Hewie sat back expectantly.

"Here, I'll give you a thousand now and you'll get the rest when the stuff is sold. Be extra careful, Slimy has big ears and we are on a good wicket. If we want to keep going, mum's the word. Now slip out quietly and put in an appearance where Dermutt can find you; the last thing we want is him getting suspicious!"

Larry handed the money across and ushered his subordinate out.

Over at the ring, where two fighters were training, Hec Stroud watched with slitted eyes as he discerned Hewie quickly exit the premises. He nudged the trainer of the two boxers.

"Eh, wasn't that the fly-boy from Sydney?"

"Huh? Who ya talkin' about?" The trainer took his eyes off his boys momentarily.

"Just thought I saw a bloke I knew, that's all!"

"Fly-boy. Ah, you mean Hewie, he's our pilot. Flies a seaplane for the boss. Larry often uses him to take our boys to our big country matches. Major country towns, we stage some good bouts in the country. Boy, do some of the yokels gamble – we get some good dough there!"

"Uh –huh, thought I knew him!" Hec said, and smiled grimly.

It was in the late morning hours that Drew Slimmery had a caller.

"Gawd! What are you doing here? Won't Larry be looking for you?" Drew asked of his visitor.

"Nah! He is busy with the two fight-boys working out their programme for the main bout tonight. They usually take about an hour trying to make it interesting for the mob. Got something important for you – guess who is in Harry's employ – a fly-boy!" Hec Stroud informed.

"A fly-boy. You are not referring to Hewie are you?" Drew asked in amazement.

"The same. Saw him nick out of Larry's office and slink away; very quickly. Thought you oughta know!" Hec said with a job well done.

"So, that is our leak? Well Mister two-faced Hewie, that spells curtains for you!"

Drew was almost apoplectic. This was a shock to him. The man he personally brought from interstate especially to help, was in the hip pocket of his worst enemy; the opposition. "That explains a lot. No wonder I was loosing my shipments. He will have to be dealt with immediately!" Drew calmed and quietly deemed.

"Want me to deal with him?" Hec asked a sneer on his normally mask-like face.

Drew cogitated for a minute, and then shook his head.

"No, you are doing a good job where you are. I don't want you to be jeopardised. I have another plan for him; two good new faces that can do away with him without bringing suspicion to us. Leave Hewie to me and get back so you won't be missed. Good work Mister Stroud, there's a bonus for you!"

Ray and Gerry were back at 'TheRiver Café' where Dermut was quietly ordering.

"Now you reckon things are a bit quiet; well, I got something for you to do!" He eyed them minutely. "You two did such a good job on Arnold that the boss has ordered that you should get a thorn out of our hides!"

"A thorn. I take it you want someone removed?" Ray asked.

"Without a trace, just make him disappear – permanently. Now that is an order right from the top!" Dermutt looked from one to the other.

"Do we get extra for it?" Gerry hedged.

The gun-runner nodded.

"Same as before – are you up to it?" Ray stroked his chin. "Who is it this time? Do we know him?" Dermutt shook his head.

"No, but he is a traitor and must be dealt with immediately, our whole cartel is in trouble with this man. He has proven to be the 'leak', that is why our goods are being interfered with. His name is Hewie and he pilots a seaplane; you know the type, one of those with floating gadgets that can be changed into wheels. You will find his plane at this strip; we will have him pick up an imaginary parcel tonight at midnight. That is when the boss wants it done!" Dermutt passed a slip of paper to Ray. "Without a trace!" Dermutt reiterated.

When the plump little man had gone, Gerry turned to Ray.

"You know what. We are getting in too deep. When they find out – we will be the next ones to be bumped off!"

"Then we had better see to it that we are not found out. The sooner we can pin the top guys with this drug and gun running; the sooner we can get out of it!" Ray said with feeling.

"How are we going to work this job out?" Gerry wanted to know.

"First we will have to speak with 'you know who'; we will be guided by what he says." Ray nodded absently, thinking.

"Well we had best get things moving – plans to make and all that." Gerry stated the obvious.

"Yes. The wives are going to be a bit toey with this one." Ray grinned and arose to go.

"Argh. They will be all right since Jason spoke with them. I really think they will be expecting us to have a night away soon!" Gerry was unperturbed.

Jason Ferguson deliberated when he was informed of the latest order given to the two storemen.

"Now, how best to approach this one?" He mused. "You two don't fly and we had better not get one of our pilots involved, Hewie may get suspicious. I think it would be best to take Hewie before he boards his plane!"

"But we do not know the man; we might grab his mechanic by mistake!" Ray worried.

"No. With a little plane like that he would do most of his own repairs – same as you do with your car – I guarantee he will be the only one at his aircraft. Now I think you should just grab him and take him for a ride same as you did before with Arnold. I will have a wagon meet you on the freeway like before and we will do something similar with Hewie. I will ring you in the morning to let you know what excuse to give Dermutt!"

"Okay, we will deliver him and await word from you!" The two made their ways home early to inform their better halves that they were needed that night.

As Hewie was preparing his aircraft for take-off, two shadowy figures crept up on him unnoticed.

"Strewth!" He exclaimed, as one of the large men held him so that he could not move his arms. The other man quickly 'frisked' him and withdrew a pistol.

"Are you 'Hewie'?" The fellow who held him asked.

"Wot if I am?" Hewie showed defiance.

"We are taking you for a ride!" Ray informed.

"You are not!" Hewie struggled futilely to escape the firm grip.

"Put a bullet in him now, and then we won't have any trouble." Gerry muttered aloud.

"Alright – okay – I won't struggle." Hewie started to panic. "Who – who sent you. Was it Dermutt?"

"Which Dermutt?" Ray asked.

"Huh? There's only one Dermutt. Dermutt Schloss; sometimes goes by the name of Berrimann – Gunther Berrimann!" Hewie was bewildered. "Now why do you think it would be Dermutt Schloss? It might have been Drew Slimmery!" Ray hedged.

"Nah. Drew wouldn't --??"

Hewie clammed up, realizing that he was implicating the big boss. Suspicions began to permeate his mind. Perhaps these were 'coppers'. Not another word could the two cajole out of him. Ray and Gerry bundled him into their vehicle and transported the unhappy man to the pre-arranged destination with the 'feds'.

Jason rang Ray as promised in the morning with news of their arrest of Hewie.

"A body was washed up on the coast yesterday." Jason informed Ray.

"Anybody that I know?" Ray asked.

"As a matter of fact it is – Charlie Orso!"

"That one of the men who took us for a ride, intending to kill us?" Ray showed his surprise.

"No, he was one of the blokes who were shadowing you. My men searched Hewie's aeroplane when you left looking for the drugs we expected him to be transporting. He had no drugs but forensic found a bullet hole that had been covered, just a fresh one, and they took some DNA samples. Charlie had been in the plane!"

"How was Charlie – er – was he killed, or was it an accidental drowning?" Ray keenly asked.

"Oh he was killed alright. Right through the skull at close quarters, even the damage by the fish could not hide that. Forensic seem to think that he may have got in Hewie's hair and Hewie could have a hand in it; anyway, Hewie is being charged with his murder!"

"Did questioning bring out anything more about the cartel?" Ray queried.

"No, I'm afraid Hewie has clammed up. We are still working on him but it does not look good. Hewie will not implicate his employers. I believe the cartel has got him scared of reprisals in the 'house'. As for you two, I think it will be better to say Hewie was arrested before you got to him; that way there is an excuse for not 'doing away' with him. You see, the underworld will get to know he is in prison. We cannot have you claiming to have done him then he turns up in prison!" Jason frowned into the 'phone.

"Okay, so I will report that Hewie did not arrive at the airstrip to fly his plane!" Ray determined.

"Sounds good. Be careful, these blokes are not stupid, you will have to be on your toes." Jason warned.

Ray rang through to Dermutt.

"I had to talk to you urgently, that there fly bloke you sent us after did not turn up. Are you sure he was going to take his aircraft out last night?"

"Eh. What do you mean he did not turn up? He had an urgent job to do – you stupid clots have let him get away!" Dermutt was furious. "You were probably too late and gave him time to go." Ray pretended that he was flabbergasted by being outwitted.

"No, he never got off the ground. His plane is still there; he just never turned up. We waited a long while but there was no sign of him!"

Dermutt went silent as he got to thinking.

"I do not know why he did not turn up for the job we arranged. I will have to speak with the boss; you two be ready to take off after him when I arrange something else. I'll meet you at 'The River Café' at lunch-time." He slammed the receiver down.

"I just don't understand it." Dermutt was excusing. "He was supposed to go and pick up a small package and my two 'hit men' says he never fronted!"

"There may be a good cause for that." Drew Slimmery pursed his lips. "I received a notice from one of my 'inside men', - just a whisper – that Hewie has been arrested and is being charged with murder. Looks like the rumour is true!"

"What?" Dermutt expostulated. "That will bugger up our pick-ups. How do we get 'round that?"

"Good question. We will just have to find another way!" Drew grimly frowned.

"Anyway." Dermutt asked. "How did you know that Hewie was the 'leak'?"

"That 'plant' that I put into Larry's camp. It paid off. Hewie was seen leaving Larry's office – in good spirits, the traitor!" Dermutt went white.

"But I thought you brought him from interstate because he was the goods!"

"Yes, so I thought too. It shows you can not trust anyone these days. One thing for sure, my man at Larry's gym is true to us and a good man to have on side." Drew smugly stated.

"Who is Hewie accused of murdering?" Dermutt asked.

"As yet, I do not know but for sure someone got in his way. Seeing that he was a traitor to our cause – look to your men. I think you will find that one of them is missing!"

"Charlie – Charlie Orso. He has not been seen since he went with Hewie to pick up that last load. Hewie reckons he heard a shot. We never found the body so I thought he was the 'leak', but it was bloody Hewie all the time!" Dermutt fumed.

"I think that you had best keep an eye on his partner – er Joe – if there is one bad egg, there could be more." Drew was revelling in the fact that one of Dermutt's men was under suspicion; after all, Drew was weakened by the fact that trusted 'Hewie', proved to be the traitor.

"Okay, I will keep an eye out, but Charlie was on our side. He got it because he was true to us – Joe is too. He might be a fumble-footed bugger but he is no traitor!" Dermutt defended his men.

"Hmmm. Probably, but do not lower your guard just the same. With the big money involved any one of your men could turn!" Drew muttered. "Dismissed!" He waved Dermutt away.

The man went but he did it in bad grace. Being blamed for something that was the fault of his boss was bad enough, being dismissed again like an errant schoolboy hurt.

"So there you have it!" Dermutt finished by saying.

"Then we do not get any extra?" Gerry bemoaned the fact.

"Never mind. There will be another time." Ray consoled. "Don't be so bloodthirsty!" Dermutt looked at his two insiders.

"Gawd! You are eager buggers. We may have to try the warehouse again now because the leak has been found. You two just be on hand and we will let you know."

Dermutt left quite satisfied that at least the cartel had two men who did not stuff things up.

Fatty Burns was in an expansive mood. Bernie Brocchio was his man for the delivery of narcotics since the demise of Charlie Orso, and both that business and the pizza shop were doing well. When word was passed on by his trusted customers that a certain code-word would get the 'good stuff' across, business began to boom. That members of the underworld began frequenting his shop did not go un-noticed by the local constabulary. This was passed on to Jason Ferguson and two undercover 'plants' were employed to find out why the underworld had a more than average interest. Two scruffy looking dead-beats got in the habit of hanging about the pizza shop, much to the annoyance of Fatty. One day he accosted them with the intent of having them 'shove off'. One of the two, sporting an uncared for goatee, with scraggly unkempt hair, belligerently took umbrage at Fatty's ordering them away.

"Awright, 'oo the hell d'ya think you are telling us to piss off?"

He leered at Fatty, who disdainfully pushed him aside. The fellow stumbled and almost fell. No doubt affected by drugs.

"Look, you two make the place untidy and I can do without you; now shove off and pollute some other shop!" Fatty ordered.

The chap with the goatee just stood swaying and looking bleary eyed at Fatty.

"Tha's nice that is. I ain't goin' until I get me a reefer. Not me – no I ain't. I come 'specially for 'em!"

"What reefers?" Fatty asked, suspiciously. The affected one dug his mate in the ribs.

"Heh. He says what reefers."

The man tried to focus on Fatty and pointed a finger.

"Smithy reckons as 'ow I can get some snort 'an that if I see the fat pri – er, bloke. I got th' dough, here look!" He fumbled though his pockets and pulled out an untidy heap of money. "There see, tha's enough ain't it?"

Fatty eyed the cash and said.

"Come around the back!"

Lieutenant Ferguson was listening intently to what his men had to say.

"So we just took the few reefers and stumbled away!"

"Okay now if you play your cards right, I think the next step is that they will try to push some 'hard' drugs onto you. Even then, do not show your hand. It is useless to just get them for petty dealing when they may lead us to someone bigger. Just get yourselves known and become 'easy' hits; that will get them off-guard.

"Yes Sir!" The scruffy looking dead-beats smartly saluted and took their leave.

CHAPTER TWELVE

Dermutt responded when Ray rang him and they were again at their mutual meeting place in 'The River Café'.

"This business associate of mine was quite pleased with the goods I got for him, only trouble was he said I was a piker. It appears that what I got was only a dribble of what he needs and he is pushing for me to get my hands on more. Is there any chance of me be able to get quite a quantity of what you gave me before?" Ray eagerly asked.

Dermutt scanned the face of this 'new' player in the game and saw only the eagerness of youth.

"I dunno – it will cost you heaps – much more than I pay you now!"

Ray was very keen.

"Argh! This sucker has got a heap, money is no barrier for him; I can take out a bank loan to cover it. He pays immediately I give him the goods!" Ray had dollar signs twinkling from his eyes.

"All right. I will see if I can get four times the amount I gave you last time – but you will have to pay me – you got that covered?" Dermutt demanded.

"Yeah – yeah, I will get a bank loan; it's in the bag!"

Larry Crumpers was talking with his head trainer.

"So, the word is that Hewie got lumbered with the murder of one of Drew's boys. The cops have him in the lock-up and it does not look like he will get out of this one. That has put a damper on our bonus trade. Pity that, we had a good thing going and the best part of it was, if anything went wrong; Slimy got lumbered for it!"

"Yair. Yer wos doin' all right from it. Ain't no hope a' getting' some other bloke from 'is mob ter 'elp is they?" The trainer said. Larry morosely shook his head.

"Nah! I could not trust another bloke like I could Hewie. We go back a long way. Do not wish to rock the boat, it could start a gang war; no, I guess we will just have to put up with it for a bit!"

Larry went quiet while he thought about it. The head trainer got up to go.

"Send Stroud in!" He called as the trainer was about to close the door.

"You wanted me Boss?" Hec Stroud came in and sat with Larry.

"Yes. I need some information. Have you heard of Drew Slimmery?"

"Huh! No. Should I?" Hec hedged.

"Just thought you may have heard a whisper about him. He runs a contraband business – you know the stuff – illegal guns and drugs; in fact any sort of contraband.

"Aw, yair. There was a whisper about him up in the northern state where I come down from, now I come to think of it – why; do you intend to do business with him?"

Larry laughed.

"Ah that would be a trick. No, what I want is to find one of his hirelings and offer him more than he gets now to come over to my mob."

"Huh! Whaffor?"

"Forewarned is forearmed." Larry said with a wink.

"Yeah, but what has that got to do with me?" Hec asked, frowning.

"You are a thinker. Most of my boys are just 'pugs', and have not got a decent brain between them. I need someone who can think for themselves. It could be dangerous, you will have to have to be cagey; think you're up to it?" Hec chucked a chest.

"'Course I can. If you want I can infiltrate their mob for you!" His smug grin giving off an air of self worth.

"No, you gotta be here to watch my back." Larry was firm in this thought.

"Now a good place to look would be with a fellow named Dermutt – er - Dermutt Schloss. He is second in the line of power. He also goes by the name of Berrimann, Gunther I think. What ever you do keep a low profile with him but he may just give you inkling as to who is working for him. You may find him at this address!"

Larry passed across a paper on which he put the information.

"Just ask Dermutt if he knows 'Fatty', he - !!"

"Fatty! You don't mean Fatty Burns?" Hec butted in.

"Why yes, do you know him?" Larry was surprised.

"Never met him, heard of him but – interstate!" Hec admitted.

"Well, I got the info that Fatty was brought down here to help with the distribution of their finished product. Find him and that will give you a good lead to a sucker who may give you the guts of what is going on. Someone who worships money more than friendship. Do you think you can do that?" Larry looked keenly at his new protector.

"No worries leave it to me!" A confident Hector Stroud said.

Drew Slimmery was in a happy mood. He had just been informed by Hec Stroud, that Larry had hired him as a 'protector', and then seconded him to try and locate a 'stoolie' that would dob in Drew and spill the beans on his shipments. They both were having a laugh at Larry's expense; along with a glass or two of fine french wine.

"Now, I have to think very deeply on this one." Drew smiled as he wiped his eyes." Who do I have in my employ that will fit the bill? Someone who knows stuff-all about me that I can use as a supposed go-between?" He gave the matter some thought, and then rang Dermutt.

"Hey, Dermutt, I got a problem. Do we have anybody on our payroll that is fairly intelligent but strapped for cash?" Drew asked in to the telephone.

"Whaffor?" Dermutt was nonplussed.

"I have Hec here and Larry wants to undermine us. He sent Hec to 'buy' one of our blokes as a traitor. The fellow will have to have a bit of intelligence because he will be a sort of double agent, selling information that we feed him to the opposition!"

"Strewth!" Dermutt gasped. "That's a bit dangerous isn't it?"

"Not if we get the right fellow – think – do we have anyone intelligent that is dispensable?"

"Gawd! I don't know. I do not think any of the pushers would be that smart. Someone dispensable? Let's see. Er – what about one of the two we have in the warehouse – they are pretty intelligent and they passed that test we hit them with; although I would not say they were dispensable. We could yet need them. But they are keen to get their mitts on cash!" Dermutt worried.

"Hey that is a good idea. We will only need one of them though. If things go wrong, well, we still have the other one to push our stuff through if we use the warehouse again; and we may need to!" Drew assented.

"Okay, send Hewie to the warehouse and ask for Ray!" Dermutt agreed.

"Jason, you said to let you know if I crossed paths with this Hec Stroud." Ray whimsically reported.

"You have met him?" Jason was amazed.

"Yes. He came around to the warehouse as bold as you like and said could he have a talk with me in private. I did not have time to get you involved and have a 'wire' set up. He called at lunch time and I took him over to the café. Guess what?" Ray did not give Jason time to guess, he went on. "Hec offered me good money, twice what Dermutt is paying, to let him know where Drew Slimmery's shipments go; and when!"

"And?"

"Well I was not about to jump at it. I told him Drew is not using us so much and I would have to think about it. Hec said 'think about it but tell no one I offered you or you will die!' I tell you what; I don't think he is kidding either!" Ray soberly said.

"Well what do you think?" Jason asked. Ray pondered a little, and then said. "I do not care; it is up to what you want."

"Drew Slimmery is not using the warehouse now and you do not really get any knowledge of his shipments anyhow. What say you tell Dermutt he is being double-crossed and see if he will work with you?" Jason suggested.

"Hec has issued a death threat will your boys be there if I need them?" Ray asked.

"My word yes, you will have a twenty four hour guard."

"Okay." Ray agreed.

When next Hec came around Ray queried.

"Yeah okay, but at the moment he is not using the warehouse if a crate comes in I will let you know first. Do I get paid now?"

"Great. No, you get paid after you tell us each time. But here is a little bit to let you know I am genuine. You remember this is just between me and you; nobody else is to know. Okay?" Hector Stroud swaggered away after paying a pittance to Ray and offering a contact number.

"Gee whiz you had better have something urgent to tell me. I have a woman waiting!" Dermutt growled.

"Yes, this is very urgent." Ray had his tongue in cheek. "I er, I had a proposition today."

"Go on." Dermutt urged. "A bloke came around to see me; he wants me to let him know when the next shipment is in for a bloke named Slimmery. I thought it may have something to do with you!" Ray carefully worded his sentences.

"Glad you told me." Dermutt nodded. "Hec is working for us. He has been hired by the opposition. We have him in there to spy on Larry Crumpers for us. He was sent over here to get one of our blokes to turn traitor and sell us out. I got him to talk to you because

I knew you were with us and you have proved that by letting me know. I will give you a bonus for staying true to our cause. Gee! You must be making a packet out of us. I'll give you information to pass on to Hec this time, though in the future we will tell him direct and he can say he got it from you. Good work Ray!"

Dermutt smiled contentedly as he went. Ray was all smiles when he reported the outcome of his venture into 'double agent' spying, to Jason Ferguson.

"So you have now firmly established your link with Dermutt, and the go-between, who is also a double agent for Slimmery will be on your side; even though he is a suspected deadly killer. We seem to be holding a trump card. When to use it to the better is now our problem." Lieutenant Ferguson could not help himself smiling grimly.

"I had better push a little harder for high quality drugs from Dermutt now, which may lead us to implicating Drew Slimmery. But what about this 'new' cartel; it would appear that they are getting involved in drugs too?" Ray asked.

"Yes, that is disturbing. Until now he has just been fight-fixing, a mob of bully boys; but drugs? He never seemed to be interested in drugs." Jason worried.

"If they pinched Slimmery's shipment from Hewie, then they could be responsible for the ouzi's that got into the hands of that radical group up in the mountains!" Ray suggested.

"Yes. We are working on that!" Jason seemed to have made up his mind. "Good work Ray. Now you get back to your post and try to implicate Drew and Dermutt, we will look after the radicals and Larry. Be always on your guard. I have got you covered all the time since we now know Hector Stroud is in the game. This is the danger time so you do not take foolish risks; that is an order." Jason frowned deeply at his new recruit.

"Yes Sir!" Ray took his leave.

Dermutt Schloss was back at Drew Slimmery's office.

"I told you our two in the warehouse were the goods!" Dermutt bragged. "Soon as Hec got to him, Ray rang and let me know we were being taken for suckers. We are pretty strong in the 'house' now. I think we can start using it again to bring our stuff in. With that bloody traitor Hewie out of it, we have to go back to our old system!"

"Yes, I suppose you are right." Drew did not sound as if he believed it was the best thing to do; however there was no other way to bring his goods into the country. "You say that this 'Ray' has a contact for high grade goods?" Drew asked.

"Why, yes!" Dermutt obliged. "And he says that he can sell heaps too."

Drew quietly thought this matter over.

"See if you can push him to take more than he wants - that way we can get him hooked and we might even have a stronger outlet. He seems to be a sensible man; use him to our advantage!" Drew ordered.

Later that day, Drew Slimmery had an Asian visitor. He was a slight man with sleek black hair. With him were two thick-set bodyguards. Drew's own body-guard, who acted as his secretary; let the trio in.

"Mister Sook Lin wants to see you, Boss." He said, ushering the three forward.

"Ah! What an unexpected pleasure gentlemen. Come in, come in!"

Drew made room for the three. The men bowed with their hands in front of them, acknowledging the invitation.

"Ah so. A preasure to see you again Mister Srimmery!"

"What makes you come over here so unexpectedly?" Drew asked a puzzled expression showing.

"There is much confusion in shipping – ah, goods – from home. Not knowing how is better ratery, you say no port then pick up at sea, now no pick-up. What happening prease?" The sleek one asked his eastern mask inscrutable.

125

"Yes. Well we were having a bit of trouble at both places. A couple of traitors in our organization. It has now been fixed up so we should have no more trouble."

Drew smiled hugely at the visitors, hoping to placate them.

"Ah so. Mister Tai Chou not wery happy about tlouble. He send me here most urgent. No can suppry if any doubt for derivery!" Sook Lin faced Drew and seemed to bore right into him. Drew Slimmery tried hard to gloss over his misfortunes. "You can pass on to Tai that everything is now in order and the merchandise is being well-distributed. Oh! And that 'special' delivery you sent; it went over quite well thank you!"

Drew's oily smile apparently made no difference, as the 'mask' did not alter.

"Will tell Mister Tai Chou you say everry sing in order now. Lemember, if more tlouble - !"

Sook Lin signed as if he was cutting a throat. He bowed with hands in front as before. The bodyguards did likewise and all took their leave.

"Phew!" Drew breathed a sigh of relief when they left. "I sure would not like to upset those three!" He told his assistant.

"Nah. Spooky!" The assistant grimaced.

Dermutt Schloss was called to the office of Drew Slimmery.

"There just better not be any more slip – ups. I had Sook Lin and his bully-boys pay a visit and they gave me a stern warning. One more stuff – up and we have had it!" His red face (enhanced by a sly nip or two) was bristling as he warned his second-in-command.

"We have to get our organization running smoothly and professionally. Tai Chou is getting very worried to send his main distributor over here personally. The man came un-announced, if they had wanted to do away with me; they could have. When the triad need to reach anyone, it just shows how easy it is for them. There is nowhere on this planet they can not reach. I tell you Dermutt, this is frightening. No more leaks, stuff-ups or distribution failures or both of our necks are on the block. Is that understood?" White – faced, Dermutt nodded.

"Sure Boss. There won't be any more stuff – ups I can assure you!"

Detective Jim Lynton, the intelligence telephone operator, came into Lieutenant Ferguson's office.
"We have struck the jackpot Sir." He reported.
"Yes?" Expectantly from Jason.
"I will just run this tape Sir." Jim did so.
After having listened, Jason applauded the diligence of his man.

"Well, Slimmery has let his hair down. Now we definitely know those three we trailed to the Air Terminal are from a triad and are the bosses of Drew and Dermutt. Both Drew and Dermutt are the main functions here for the triad and now we are sure who the heads are in Asia. Getting solid proof that will stand up in court are now our major concerns!" Jason happily smiled. Detective Lynton asked.
"Knowing that this Sook Lin is the importer and Tai Chou may be the head of the triad, is not enough on its own Sir; we need to come up with something concrete. How do you propose we do that?"
"Yes!" Mused Jason. "How indeed!"
"Contact their 'tail' at the air port and have the forward destination secured. The International boys can pick them up from their home terminal and have them monitored so that we know where their base is; the International blokes probably already know of them anyway. But we have to be sure so that they can be trapped!" Jason ordered.
"Yes Sir!" Detective Lynton departed to consummate his orders.
Detective Sergeant Graeme Carey, who was an interested bystander; asked.
"Do you suppose we could get this Ray to play a higher profile than he already has?"

"We may get the big brass on our backs if we push the young fellow any harder. After all, he is basically a civilian still you know!" Jason worried.

"But it is imperative that we push the advantage we have right now." Graeme stressed.

"Yes. We will have to secure the Asian connection before we close Drew and Dermutt down, otherwise they would just get some other cartel to push their wares here." Jason thoughtfully mused.

Dermutt was in 'The River Café' as arranged with Ray.

"When you rang I barely had time to get here!" Ray excused. "That is why I was a little late. Lucky I got the bank loan yesterday so I had it on hand."

"You got the cash? I do not take bank cheques." Dermutt keenly enquired.

"No cheques. Crisp new bank notes. You better have the good stuff, my associate only wants quality!" Ray emphasised, feeling that the big cash he had on hand made him a little more authoritarian.

"Yeah, this is top quality – let me see the money first!"

Ray slipped across an envelope. Carefully looking about before he opened it, Dermutt greedily counted the cash.

"Yep! Correct weight!"

Dermutt pushed forwards the brief-case he had and said, under his breath.

"Just look at what you bought but don't take it out of the case. Someone could be watching." Ray did so. He arose to go.

"No! I will go first, you wait awhile!" Dermutt cautioned.

He got to the door when two plain clothed men took him under arrest. As he struggled with them he caught a glimpse of Ray likewise being apprehended. The briefcase was nowhere to be seen.

CHAPTER THIRTEEN

"Detectives Max Riley and Frank Dean reporting Sir."

The two saluted as they came into the office of Lieutenant Ferguson.

"At ease gentlemen." Jason ordered.

He sat in his chair and offered the detectives take a seat.

"So, caught Dermutt red-handed with the marked cash in hand and the drugs in his brief-case with his prints bold as brass; eh? Good work!"

"Yes Sir. And the 'wire' Mister Cress wore has his voice clear as a bell Sir!" Max Riley affirmed.

"And what of the cassette?" Jason asked.

"The man behind the one-way glass in the back room said that he filmed the change-over well but Mister Schloss was half turned and did not fit the frame properly. The coverage will be just so-so as evidence!" Max apologised.

"Never mind, what we have will be damning enough. Now, did Dermutt see Ray being arrested?" Jason raised his eyebrows.

"I made sure that he got a good look and Frank had the cuffs in plain view Sir."

"So!" Jason nodded. "He thinks that Ray got arrested too; did you have the other car there?"

"Yes Lieutenant. Mister Schloss was informed that his accomplice was being taken to headquarters for a grilling!"

"Good!"

"Sorry Mister Stroud, I did not know who else to contact." Ray excused when he was at last face-to-face with the 'hit-man', at 'The River Café'.

"So you located a shipment did you?" Hec asked his ferret-like eyes boring in to Ray's worried face.

"No – not a shipment – I er, I had to let you know that my boss; Dermutt, has been arrested. So --!!"

"What? Dermutt arrested. When, what happened?"

"This morning. I was just about to buy some good stuff off him when the drug squad moved in; they must have followed him. I got lumbered too, but I never had any money on me and the stuff was still in the case where he left it; lucky it was still where he sat. I told them it had nothing to do with me. I said he was trying to sell the stuff to me but I did not want anything to do with it. As I had no money on me and no drugs either, they had to let me go!" Hec bored right at Ray, trying to find the answer.

"What made you come to me; I warned I would kill you if you crossed me. Don't you know I work for the opposition?" Hec gave Ray a steely look.

"Yes, I know. But as I am honest with my employer I told Dermutt about you. He said it was all right, you are working for us, so, as I don't know who Dermutt's boss is; I thought I would take the risk and ask you!"

Hec looked long and hard at Ray, whose heart was pumping with the risk he was taking.

"Yeah!" Hec said. "You done right. This is a 'mergency, I will let the boss know, good work Ray, I'll let you know what to do next; just sit tight and wait 'til I get back to you!" Hector Stroud swaggered away.

Ray was not at all sure just how safe he was. That the man he had just spoken with was a time bomb about to go off, he had no doubt. The big storeman went back to the real job he had after notifying Jason of what had transpired.

Ashen-faced, Drew listened to his confidant.

"So evidently this Ray pushed the case of stuff under the chair that Dermutt was in, and got out of it. He must have already given the dough to Dermutt and not having the goods and no money – they could do nothing!" Hec smiled a sickly smile. "That is quick thinking. I woulda done the same."

"Blast the rotten luck. Dermutt is a key man; I'll get my barrister to see can we get him bailed." Drew cursed. "Now we are in a pickle, I have not got a replacement for Dermutt!"

"I could take over for him; 'course I'd haveta quit working for Larry."

Hec suggested. Drew looked at him; then shook his head.

"No, you are too valuable where you are – I could not replace you there. I have to have a man I can trust in Larry's employ. Lemme think a minute!" He leaned back in his chair to cogitate. Hec politely remained silent.

"I thought of Fatty, but he is better at doing what he is doing – no – I had best leave him put. Other than you and Fatty there is no one else to fill Dermutt's shoes. We will just have to see what the barrister comes up with; he might get Dermutt off!"

"What about one of the pushers, surely there is someone there who can fill in for a bit?" Hec asked.

"No, I would not trust a shovel full of them, they are not thinkers. Most of them would sell their mother if the price was right. The top men are in the distribution outlets. I can't take one of them away – I'd only get a frump to replace them – no, I need Dermutt; Damn it!"

"This Ray is a good thinker; would he do?" Drew looked keenly at Hec.

Hesitation on his worried brow.

"He is too new; I do not even know the man. I know Dermutt speaks highly of him but I don't know. He has a pretty solid job at the warehouse by all reports."

Drew drummed on his desk with his fingers.

"Money talks all languages. By the sound of it, this Ray is hungry for money and the 'feds' got a haul of his when they took Dermutt. Ray is not going to claim that because it will implicate him. He probably owes for it!" Hec surmised.

Drew stared at his next in line, thinking.

"Tell you what-" Drew pursed his lips "- bring this 'Ray' in so I can speak with him. Blindfold him so he won't remember where I have my office. I will sound him out!" Drew had made up his mind to at least see what sort of a man he had working for him.

"Yeah. I do not think you will be let down. He seems a very sensible chap; and he will be easy to manipulate. I will bring him up after he knocks off tonight."

Hec said, rising to go.

"No – bring him in after dark – someone may notice the blindfold otherwise."

Drew stopped Hec in his tracks.

"Oh yeah, I will arrange it and bring him in about nine. I should not be missed by Larry then for an hour!" Hec left.

Ray was at Jason Ferguson's office.

"I think we have got a foot in the door." Ray said. Jason attentatively listened. "Hec Stroud called at work just as I was leaving. He wants to pick me up there at eight-thirty sharp. Something about a promotion but he could not say any more!"

Ray raised his eyebrows in a questioning manner.

"Hmmm. I do not like it; he is a killer by all reports. I do not like it; maybe you should not go?" Jason worried.

"If I do not have a 'wire' and I am un-armed, the risk is minimal. This may be our big chance if this promotion is legit!" Ray emphasised.

"If – if, that is the problem. I cannot take the risk of putting a civilian in the line of fire!" Jason shook his head. "But if – there is that word again – if it is a genuine chance for you to be promoted higher into the cartel. Well I have to take the bull by the horns to stop this influx of dope and guns into the country. We should at least have a signalling device to monitor your position!" Jason had made up his mind.

"Tell you what –" Ray suggested "- I would rather not have anything on my person, because if I am caught with it; then I will be a candidate for being done away with. We know I may have to front Slimmery, as we know where his office is; why don't I take a small device and leave it under the seat in Hec's vehicle. That way, when the trace stops you will know where I am. I am sure it will stop at Slimmery's office."

"All right, we will do it your way; after all, you are the one taking the risk. Are you sure you're up to it?" Jason persisted.

"Leave it to me!" Ray as usual, exuded confidence.

"Well, here he is Boss!" Hec nudged the big man forward.

Ray nodded to Drew Slimmery. It was the first meeting that he had with the tall thin man and Ray was surprised at his immaculate attire.

"You had the blindfold on?" Drew asked.

"Sure Boss, just like you said; I took it off when he was inside the building."

"You understand Mister Cress, that I must make these necessities as a precaution; I have much to lose so it is just a safe-guard. Dermutt speaks well of your work for our cause, you have a contact who wants only good quality?" He studied Ray's reaction.

"Yes, I do." Ray barely answered.

"Is it someone I should know?" The question was pointed.

"No!" Drew paused and with finger on nose, pondered.

"I see. You tried to purchase a quantity of high grade off Dermutt. What went wrong?"

It was Ray's turn to phrase his answer carefully.

"It would appear that he was 'tailed' to our meeting. I paid him the money and he was satisfied. I saw the goods but only briefly.

When the raid was on I quickly dropped the case to the floor and pushed it with my foot to where Dermutt was sitting. No use the two of us getting busted!" He looked defiantly at Drew.

Darkly, Drew peered at Ray.

"You realise that Dermutt was a crucial cog in my network?"

"Stiff shit!" Ray quietly said. "Look after number one is my motto. He let the 'feds' follow him there, he can take the rap!"

The fearless way this new man stood up to him impressed Drew Slimmery.

"Do you think you can take over Dermutt's work?" The question was most unexpected.

"Huh?" Ray looked amazed. "I thought I was being brought here to let you know what happened; I – er, I did not expect to be offered his job!" Ray explained, apparently much flustered.

"You were highly recommended by Dermutt. I can see that you are not just a run-of-the-mill drug pusher and you carry yourself with authority. I need such a man in my organization; are you in?"

Ray gave the impression of one who had just won the lottery.

"Do I have to give up my day job?" He asked.

"No. I am sure we can work around that – less suspicion that way – you may have to do a little overtime away from your workplace though!"

"Yes Mister Slimmery. Where do I start?" Ray was very subservient.

Drew turned to Hector Stroud.

"Leave us and get back to your post Hec, I believe Ray and I can work things out now. Dismissed!"

The man went without so much as a by-your-leave; he had done what was required of him. Drew put his attention entirely on his new man.

"Now, I have had a visit from my higher ups. They have warned me that they do not want any more stuff-ups." Drew let that sink in, and then continued.

"They are unaware that Dermutt has been apprehended, not that they knew him very well, but it is imperative that they do not find out; are you with me?" "Yes Boss!" "Good. Now Dermutt was preparing some finished products to go to Fatty Burns at our new outlet. It is a Pizza Shop down town; here is the address. I know he had a Bernie Brocchio delivering the goods but I doubt if you can find him. Wait a minute!" Drew shuffled through his papers. "Ah, here it is. I will just run a copy of this off"- he did so –"now guard that with your life. It has the contacts you will need on it!"

"Is there a time-table for deliveries?" Ray asked.

"No, when a quantity becomes available then the distribution points are notified when they can expect a delivery. If you are not one hundred percent sure; hold the delivery. We work on a cash basis, so I will expect you to make the returns to me immediately – is that understood?"

"Yes Mister Slimmery. Now these other addresses are all drop-off points?" Ray surmised.

"No, not all of them; some are reliable men who work for me. Do not trust any of them with vital information. Have you got that covered?" Drew asked, peering deeply into his new man's eyes.

"Yes Sir Mister Slimmery." Ray was shown the door with a friendly slap on the shoulder.

Jason was not at his office when Ray dutifully reported back after his late meeting with the top man of the cartel. A message was left and Ray went home to his faithful, although very worried, wife. Cindy was glad to see her man back home safe and well.

"It has been a worrying time for me lately dear!" She said as she fondly hugged and kissed her other half.

"Ah! I am so sorry Sweet, to put you through all of this - but someone has to do it - and I am the best man for it at the moment. Never mind, it should soon be over and we can get back to a 'normal' life!" He kissed her again, and then asked. "How about a cuppa Love, I sure could do with it; I have had a harrowing time of it lately."

"Oh you poor Dear. You sit back and read the papers or something; I will make you a nice cup of coffee – anything to eat?" She called from the kitchen.

"No thanks Sweet, just a drink and your warm company!"

Ray had barely arisen the next morning when an early visitor came a-knocking.

"Oh! Mister Ferguson. Please come on in!" Cindy answered the door. "Coffee?"

"Yes please, that would be great." He answered. "Had to catch you early to find out how Ray went yesterday. I received his message late last night and deemed it better to see him this morning. Do not want to blow his cover too much by risking him at the station!" Lieutenant Ferguson smiled.

"Are you sure you have him properly protected?" Cindy worried.

"Rest assured we can not protect him too much, he is now an integral part of our set-up; an extremely important part. I hope you realize how very great a part he is playing for us all. His country owes him a great deal. Ray will be remembered as a major pawn in one of the greatest games this country has played!" Jason nodded.

"Oh. That sounds so morbid, as if he was past. My husband is alive and well!"

Cindy placed coffees for all about the table.

"Yes, yes, of course. I meant it in the nicest way. Ray would be a fine detective you know."

"Really? Ah, here he is now. Mister Ferguson has popped in."

Cindy welcomed her lover with a morning kiss.

"Please, call me Jason. We do not have to be so formal privately!" Jason said.

"Good morning Sir. As it turned out, I could have worn a 'bug'; they never frisked me at all." Ray greeted.

"And what happened, did you get to see the big fellow?" Jason was eager to know.

"Better!" Ray had a mischievous grin.

"Better!" Jason was surprised. "How better?"

"I was given that promotion we were keen to see. You are now speaking to the second-in-command of the wing of the cartel!" Ray elaborated. "I do hope you are suitably impressed." Jason sat with mouth almost agape.

"Impressed? I am flabbergasted. Second only to Slimy. You are a wizard, how did that come about?" His wide eyed stare begged a quick explanation.

"Right man at the right time, getting Dermutt trapped was the key, Slimmery was left without a thinker – he says his pushers are not brainy enough to do the manipulating of people – he needed a more intelligent bloke for Dermutt's job. As Dermutt spoke highly of me; well, no one on his payroll who was any good could be spared. So, at a pinch because I was reliable – here I am!" Ray grinned as a Cheshire cat.

"Well done." Jason applauded. "Now, we have to plan this well.

"From what I can see of it Slimmery has been hit hard of late, so he is in a very vulnerable position. I really believe that is one of the reasons that he is trying a new man, fresh approach, brains and a new vigour – you know – rustle up some new style to keep his army of miscreants in a state of awareness!" Ray commented.

"Yes, it could be. Now let us go over the situation. Slimmery heads the cartel with Dermutt as his aide, Dermutt has been apprehended and a new man (yourself) has been given his responsibilities. Of his four or five shipments that we know of, only one or possibly two have got through. He is grossly understaffed. One of his pushers, that er – Luntz, Bert Luntz – has been arrested along with Dermutt (his second-in-command) and another known pusher, Charlie Orso; has been shot. Behind bars we also have a key man in Hewie, the seaplane pilot. Now Slimmery is worrying how to get his shipments in unmolested. If we have not been intercepting them, then the other cartel is; that is a worry. They are supplying these rebels with high powered ouzis and other arms that Drew ordered in; what this other cartel is doing with the drugs side of their haul – who knows. We have to find out!" Jason stopped for a breather. "Then we have this new outlet of a pizza joint that my men are working on at the moment. Hopefully that is just an outlet; anyway, we seem to have it covered. Some way we have to get them caught red-handed but not jeopardise you. That will take some very skilful handing. How are you coping so far?"

Jason was serious and genuinely concerned about the implication he was putting this 'civilian' through.

"I am fine – so is Gerry – we can handle it!" Once again Ray exuded confidence.

"Yes, so you keep saying but I do worry just the same; we are playing for high stakes here. Do not forget – no, never forget – these people are reckless with someone else's life. Do not make mistakes and do not take foolish risks. Those are orders!"

"Yes Sir!"

"Now your main job is to find out when the next delivery is to be picked up and where it's destination is, who and how many men are involved and where it will be better to trap the big pins. If somehow you can get Slimmery involved, well that is the main aim of this exercise. We do not want the big banana to get away. He keeps himself well covered." Jason drummed his fingers again as was his habit. "It may be best to let any small dribbles through so that we can concentrate on a major hit. I cannot have you risk throwing your cover for a few reefers. Have you got that?"

He peered long and urgently at his protégé.

"Everything will be fine. Trust me!" Ray promised his face serious.

CHAPTER FOURTEEN

"You wanted to see me?" Ray asked as he addressed Drew Slimmery after having sat down.

"Yes." The big man said, looking through a sheaf of papers which he took great pains to make sure that they could not be indirectly perused by his new off-sider. "Something big has cropped up (not by accident, I might add) and you have to be very careful that the information I am going to give you, does not leave this office!"

His piercing gaze bored right into the new second-in-command.

"The largest shipment that has ever come my way is being brought in by private plane at two-thirty tomorrow morning." The unwavering gaze kept on Ray. "You are to arrange it's pick-up at this farm" – he placed a slip of paper for Ray's perusal – "and it will be best to take a couple of Dermutt's trusted men to give you a hand." Drew waited as Ray looked at the address, then he screwed the paper up and disposed of it. "There will be four crates – better take one of my works vans – I want no incompetence what-so-ever. Slick receipt of the goods, delivery, and quiet dispersal. There are small arms, silencers, two crates of hard stuff and the smaller one is for

Fatty when it has been processed. These crates are worth quite a few millions and you pay with you life if they go astray!"

Ray nodded grimly denoting that he understood.

"Where do you want them delivered to?"

He quietly said, as if it were just a message to take around the corner.

"They will be best dropped off at the Richmond plant now that the feds have given it a thorough going over. That is the last place they will be expecting a delivery to!"

Drew smiled smugly.

"There is only one small problem." Ray explained. "Who is the person I ensure is the right one at the plant. I don't know them?"

"Ah yes. Good point. You had best determine that a 'Carl Schliffler', takes the goods from you – he is likely to be the only one there so early anyway. I have instructed him to be on hand!" Drew informed.

"Right Mister Slimmery, it is as good as done!" Ray confidently stated.

Drew stopped Ray's exit.

"Remember, this is a costly cargo – take no risks and move swiftly but without too much haste. We do not wish to draw attention to what is happening!"

"Yes Boss!" Ray departed.

"Where have you been?" Larry urgently wanted to know of Hec, as he casually walked into the Gym.

"Had to pick up some fodder for my 'piece', I can only get it from one source down here; it's a special size!" Hector Stroud's steely gaze penetrated his employer's.

Larry grunted, and then mused. 'We have nicked a couple of shipments off of Slimy'. He eyed Hec furtively. Then directly to the man he queried.

"That was good business for us, now that we have lost our best ever go-between, there is a bit of a gap in my organization. I only wish that I had a good fill-in, Hewie is hard to replace! I do not suppose you would know of a likely candidate for his replacement, would you?" His slitted eyes tried to fathom Hec's response.

"Nah! Do you want I should sort of wiggle in to their mob and see if I can find out?" The gunman asked, matter-of-factly. Larry was silent while he did some heavy thinking, and then shrugged his shoulders.

"Better to wait a bit yet, I still have my man working on the last lot of 'lollies' trying to break it down for sale."

"Where have you got the stuff stashed?" Hec asked. Larry looked at him.

"It's quite safe!"

"Ay! I just remembered!" Hec announced. "There is a bloke who just may be able to help out in that direction." Larry had a somewhat bemused expression.

"Yeah?"

"No really, this bloke is a confidante of Dermutt's. Now that Dermutt is out of it – he will be wondering where his next quid is coming from; he should be ripe for picking!"

Hec showed a little enthusiasm.

"Who is he?" Larry wanted to know.

"I think he is the storeman in charge of the customs warehouse. I know Dermutt used to confide in him and tell him what shipments to push through; Slimy will have to get someone else to instruct him now. If we get to the bloke first, give him more than Slimy does, I reckon he could tell us when and where the next shipment is!"

Hec affected an air of bravado. Larry absently nodded his agreement.

"And what makes you think he will do that, he might just as easily report to whoever his next boss is and blow it for us?"

"If he won't work for us – I will blow him away!" Hec quietly promised.

And so it was arranged for Hec to approach Ray and get him to divulge when and where the next shipment would be. But first and most importantly, Hector Stroud had urgent cause to visit Drew Slimmery.

"You must have something important to tell me, as you have only just recently left here!" Drew surmised when he let Hec into his office.

"Yeah!" Hec slouched into a chair. Drew patiently awaited the man's news.

"You was right!" Hec grinned. "I got it right from the horse's mouth. Larry and his mob have been intercepting your stuff all right. Hewie was their best man, he was the informer who got into the cartel and told Larry when each shipment was due and he dropped them off for Larry!"

"Yes. I knew that already." Drew again waited.

"Well, Larry has a man 'cutting' your drugs right now; he would not tell me where, I asked. Will I put a slug in him?" Hec asked.

Drew frowned as he shook his head.

"No, not yet, we will have to see can we locate my missing goods first. How come you got away?"

"Larry sent me to get your new man Ray on his side. Wants me to bribe him and have him tell when your next shipment is in; and where!"

"Ah. This is too good to be true!" Drew remarked, a very satisfied grin upon his normally serious features. "Now let me think a minute, this will have to be good!"

Hec patiently sat with immobile face as his superior cogitated. Absently nodding to himself, Drew finally had made up his mind on a course of action.

"Okay. Let Larry know that you spoke with Ray and he said that a big crate of guns and drugs is being dropped off at our country farm. Tell him they are automatic rifles, very modern, and that drugs of high quality will be used as packing. That way I will only need one crate. Er – let us see – tell him that at two on Thursday morning it is expected to touch down. I will get our demolition man to put in a powerful blast that is set to detonate at two-fifteen; that should put them somewhere on the country road leading to the freeway!" Hec had a huge grin on his face as he heard the plan.

"That should give our Larry a shock. Wonder if I can kid him into being there?"

Hec surmised.

"Tell him that I personally want to cover this one because too much of my stuff is going astray; that should get him there!" Drew cunningly supplied.

Ray dutifully had Bernie Brocchio pick up and deliver some reefers and smack to Fatty. Although it was more than a 'small amount' as described by Jason, he fulfilled his obligation. The 'hidden' task force would 'mop up' when he was clear. Ray of course, knew nothing of Drew Slimmery's plot to thwart Larry Crumpers. He blissfully went about his duties. In the interim, the 'Mod Squad' were in force and overwhelmed Fatty's pizza shop. The two scruffy-looking dead-beats were finally allowed to show their hands. Heading the mod squad, they thoroughly went over Fatty Burn's shop and their combing finally uncovered the illicit drugs and an amount of money. Fatty Burns was taken into custody with the damning evidence being very difficult to explain. He and his co-workers were arrested and the pizza shop closed down. The cooks and delivery man were later cleared of any wrong-doing; they were freed. Bernie Brocchio was not implicated as he had delivered the goods and was long gone. Joe Ratt answered the door at Ray's knocking.

"Geez!"

He exclaimed as he recognised one of the men he and Bert Luntz were supposed to have done away with. As Bert made a snatch for his pistol, Ray expecting the move, acted before the weedy stand-over man had made good his attempt. He was thrust up against the wall with the weight of the bigger man leaning upon him and his right arm twisted in a 'hammer lock' behind his back. Ray spoke quietly and calmly in the little man's ear.

"What is it like to be on the other end of gun?"

"I was following orders!" Bert mumbled.

"And you will keep on following orders too; I have taken over from Dermutt; have you got that?" Ray spoke with authority.

"Huh?" Bert puzzled.

"Dermutt has been sprung selling stuff and he is in the cooler. Slimy has me as his second-in-command. I give the orders now and you will obey them same as you did with Dermutt; is that understood?" Ray demanded.

"But Dermutt was the one who ordered that you and that other bloke should be got rid of!" Bert argued.

"That was before I joined the cartel. Dermutt and I are good associates now, we worked together. He is out of it so the boss has asked me to take over on Dermutt's recommendation. You and I have got to work together so forget about doing me in and listen. The boss wants me to pick up a big consignment of goods for him and I have to take a couple of Dermutt's men to help; you are one!"

"Okay. Lemme down, I'm listening." Bert straightened his clothing. "Who else is helping?"

"Bernie Brocchio; do you know him?" Ray asked.

"Yeah!" Bert nodded.

"Right. Now I need for you to pick up one of Slimmery's vans, get Bernie and wait for me at the corner of High and Main at one on Tuesday morning. We have to pick the gear up at the country farm. Have you got that?" Ray urgently peered at Joe to gauge his acceptance of this situation suddenly thrust upon him. Again Bert nodded.

"Slimy said 'no slip-ups', so be there on time and keep it quiet!"

Ray departed, smiling grimly.

At two o'clock on the night Ray was to deliver the goods at the Richmond Plant, the Federal Police took Carl Schiffler in for questioning. To his pleas that he had to be at the Factory for an urgent interstate delivery, the arresting officers turned a deaf ear. He was held overnight.

"Mister Slimmery?" Ray spoke through the receiver.

"Yes, that you Ray?"

"Yes. Where is this Carl Schliffler? There is absolutely no one around – not a soul – I can not just leave this consignment here unattended. What do you want I should do with it?" Silence greeted his remarks. Drew asked.

"Are you sure? Carl is usually very reliable with an important delivery like this. Have another look, he must be about somewhere!"

"No. Both Bert and I have thoroughly searched the premises. Not a sign of anybody, I think he must have forgotten or something!"

"Hang on a minute; I will ring his home address." There was silence for a while, and then Drew could be heard picking up the 'phone. "Damn! He is not answering at home. Have another look around."

"Yes Boss!" Ray hung up. Ten minutes later he rang Drew again. "No – he is just not here. Will I deliver the stuff to somewhere else?" Ray worried.

Again there was quiet as Drew cogitated.

"No, hang on for a few minutes; I will bring over some keys. Wait quietly until I get there. Do not bring any attention to yourselves, I will not be long!" He hung up.

Within ten minutes a smart little sports sedan purred up to the waiting Slimmery's Toy Factory van loaded with contraband and the three men Drew Slimmery had working for him.

"He has not turned up yet?" Drew asked of Ray.

"No Sir, Mister Slimmery. We have looked thoroughly about the place. He just is not here!"

"Well I will open the factory for you. Bring the goods in here." Slimmery ordered.

"Did you get four crates?" Ray nodded in the affirmative.

"Yes Sir. This here crate is the small one that has to be 'cut' for Fatty; is it not?"

Drew looked at it. "Yes, yes. Put it over here. That one will be the weapons and these two are the 'hard' stuff. I may as well check it is the goods that I ordered while I am here!" Drew Slimmery picked up a hammer from a work bench close by and opened the crate. Neatly packed were blocks of uncut chemical for treatment. There were hundreds of them.

"Ahh! That is a sight!" He drooled.

"Police! Keep your hands in the air and don't move!"

Lights flooded the area as Drew Slimmery disappeared behind a partition. The three remaining men were arrested and charged with possession of narcotics and firearms. The four crates were taken into police custody and the factory declared a crime scene. Drew Slimmery was not found although a thorough search of factory and grounds was made. The search for him was hotted up. Another load of Special Forces was hurriedly ordered in to continue looking for the main man. His disappearance became a fast growing topic of controversy. When Joe Ratt and Bernie Brocchio were hustled into the divvy van, Jason took Ray aside and they briefed each other upon the night's work.

"Got any ideas about where Slimmery got to Ray?" Jason worried.

"No, I would like to see behind that partition though."

"We have thoroughly searched there; still, another look will not hurt." Jason smiled.

Behind the partition a doorway led into another room of the factory.

"He must have gone through this doorway and found another exit from the factory somehow!" Jason stated the obvious.

Ray retraced their steps and looked again behind the partition.

"This wall is panelled. I just wonder if it is solid." He mused, thumping the wall with his clenched fist. A dull thud was all the satisfaction he got.

"It is just a wall!" Jason said as he too thumped the wall.

"Yes!" Ray agreed, although not really convinced. He went to where the door was and peered into the room the other side of the wall.

"Do my eyes deceive me or am I imagining things."

"Eh?" Jason exclaimed. "What do you mean?"

"This room, it does not seem as deep as the passage is long!" Ray explained.

Jason peered at the room and then judged for himself the distance of the passageway behind the partition.

"By jove. You could be right!"

Both men hurried to thump the wall beyond the room's extension. As they thumped along the wall to the steady reverberation of dull thuds. Eventually the dull thuds were replaced by a high pitched rattle.

"Bingo!" Jason remarked. "There must be a lever somewhere, or a moveable object!"

The two pored over the panelling amid the ever increasing spectators as more of the squad wondered just what the two were up to.

"Looking for finger-prints." The Sergeant smilingly asked. His mile changed to a look of wonder as Jason suddenly found the trigger which allowed the panel to open.

"Now is the time to look for finger-prints!" He smiled, entering the passageway beyond. It was not hard to find a light-switch and the illuminated passage delved deep below the factory.

"Right, just the Sergeant and Ray, come with me. The rest of you men get back to your duties!" Jason ordered.

"Yes Sir!"

The rest of the squad departed leaving the three to continue the chase for the elusive leader of the cartel. The passageway kept going on a gradual decline until it became obvious that they were below the factory floor. Another door, this one made of metal and quite rusty, was set into what appeared to be a sewage outlet; the smell quite horrific. The door had a heavy and well-rusted latch. It seemed to be hand fashioned as if it was a make-shift appliance. A heavy spanner was lying on the ground nearby but was not needed as the door was ajar. The trio entered the smelly sewer.

"My hat!" Jason ejaculated, covering his nose with a handkerchief.

The other two did likewise. They followed the outlet to its exit in the river which flowed some half a kilometre from the factory.

"Well, it looks like our quarry has got away!" The sergeant voiced what was in the minds of his companions.

"It would appear so. Let us go to the factory in the fresh air." Jason urged.

The three set out through the narrow lanes and streets.

"The problem is now that Slimmery has slipped through our fingers, your cover might be blown Ray. It just depends what reports he gets from the 'inside', no doubt he will have lots of hidden talent there; it may be best if we have you seen to be brought in as part of the cartel. Are you up to it?" Jason suggested. Ray agreed.

"Whatever you think is best. We have to make it look like I was arrested with Joe and Bernie; otherwise with Drew getting away I will not be safe!"

It was still early morning and quite dark as the men left the sewage drain to return to the factory. From the upstairs balcony of a nearby block of flats, Drew Slimmery was an interested spectator as he peered through the darkness trying to determine who were the members of the search party who disgorged from the outlet. His eyes tried desperately to distinguish just who the largest of the three men were but could not positively name him. With dire thoughts he hurried away.

CHAPTER FIFTEEN

Hector (Hec) Stroud was urgently summoned into Drew Slimmery's office.

"Yeah, what is the problem?" The cunning little man asked.

"It would appear that you have made a monumental mistake!" Drew glanced through slitted eyes at his subordinate. "That big shipment of mine has crashed. It was set up by the 'feds' and I suspect that one of your recommendations has a lot to do with it. I am not absolutely sure but I was nearly caught up in their trap and it was triggered by your new man Ray; I think!" Hec visibly paled at the accusation.

"But – but he was recommended by Dermutt!" Hec stammered.

"So you say – but the facts are becoming clearer lately. Dermutt was trapped, Ray was present but he 'got off' through a technicality. He also arranged for 'Fatty' to have a good delivery of 'goods'; now I have word that Fatty has been apprehended and his shop closed down. It would appear that this 'Ray' of yours is right in the thick of all my problems." Hec just listened but said nothing.

"When I escaped the trap by the feds, I waited to see who the pursuers were." Drew snarled. "There was a large man amongst them, and I fancy he was this Ray of yours. Your immediate job is to see that he does not interfere in my affairs again!"

"Sure thing Boss. It is as good as done!"

Dermutt Schloss was in a cell all by himself. He was cursing the rotten luck that put him there. 'I wonder why Ray did not get arrested too.' Was the uppermost question in his mind? Then a commotion was heard and the cell door was opened. Ray was unceremoniously shoved in with Dermutt.

"There, you blokes deserve each other!" The jail warden hissed.

Ray dusted himself down as he muttered.

"Flipping animals, they treat a man like dirt. I bet they have something to hide – they just have not been caught yet!" Dermutt was wide-eyed.

"I wondered where you got to, what did you say?"

Ray gave the appearance that he hated the prison authorities.

"Ah! The blithering idiots. I got off that other business when you were picked up – I had no money on me and no drugs either; I pushed the drugs under your chair when the coppers raided the café. They had to let me go!" He spat out.

Dermutt looked at him in disbelief.

"Then how come you got picked up?" Ray looked blue murder out of the cell bars. There appeared to be no one listening. He informed Dermutt of his latest escapade.

"There must still be a 'leak' in your organization. When you were taken out of it, I took over your place and was delivering the stuff. I got one shipment to Fatty and the boss got me to pick up a big one from the farm. I delivered that one to this 'Carl Schiffler' but he was not there where he was supposed to be. I think the rat 'dobbed', 'cause the 'feds' made a bust and raided the Richmond joint again. That is when they got me. Slimy let us in when we could not find Carl. Dunno if he got caught or not!" Ray brooded, looking for the entire world as if he had lost everything.

"What was Slimy doing opening up the factory? Normally he would not be caught dead anywhere near a shipment!" Dermutt puzzled.

Ray casually glanced at his accomplice.

"When we got there with the goodies, and no Carl, there was no way we could just leave the stuff there. I rang the boss and he came to open up for us."

"Do you think the boss got caught?" Dermutt asked, incredulously.

"Didn't see him, maybe he got away." Ray sulked.

The two spent half a day together, then they were disturbed in the afternoon. Two wardens came and took Dermutt away.

"Okay come with us, you two are to be separated!"

At nightfall when all prisoners were locked in their cells, Ray was given his liberty. He was picked up outside the prison by Jason.

"Well. How did it go?" The Lieutenant asked.

"Seems like word will get around now that I have been apprehended. I made sure Dermutt thinks that I was busted when the Richmond raid was on; I just hope that word gets to Slimmery!" Ray worried.

"Lay low for a couple of days. You should be safe enough at work; we know that the cartel is not using the warehouse at present so there should not be any spies about." Jason grinned.

"We will have to work on getting me a good excuse for not being 'inside', if any of Slimmery's men sights me I could become a target!" Ray frowned.

"Yes, we are working on that at present. Just keep a low profile and I will have our legal men work something out!"

Because he had been absent for a couple of hours each day, due to the commitments he found necessary with his ties to the cartel; Ray was obliged to put in a few hours overtime to make up the shortfall. Gerry was privy to his arrangements and covered for Ray at work, however, as Ray was the foreman; there were some duties that needed his personal and physical presence. Therefore he was leaving the office to go home in the dark of the evening. There were only a couple of cars left in the car parking area and as Ray was about to enter his vehicle; there on the ground was a five dollar note.

"Lucky little me!" He murmured to himself as he stooped to gather it up. The ominous ricochet of a bullet glancing off the roof of his vehicle had Ray immediately duck behind it.

"Strewth!" He ejaculated. "That was too close. That was a lucky note all right!"

Ray glanced to the direction which the bullet had come from. There was little noise from the shot, just a dull thump no doubt because a silencer was used. It was not immediately obvious who had taken a pot-shot at him but Ray had no doubt that his termination was ordered by Drew Slimmery. It was also possible that Hec was the attempted assassin. Ray was immobile, looking earnestly around for the slightest movement to denote the whereabouts of the gunman. He kept low, edging around to the other side of his vehicle. Eyes ever alert. He had opened the car door and momentarily stood up to enter the vehicle, when he spotted the flash of a revolver just as another bulled whizzed by alarmingly close. Hopping quickly into his car he set the vehicle zigzagging towards the flash which came from the roof of a nearby factory, closed for the day. Ray quit his car and ran around to the rear of the building where he knew there were some steps leading to the top floor of the two storied building. No one was in sight.

He remained quite still, waiting for his assailant to descend. For fifteen minutes all was quiet. Ray waited patiently. Perhaps the sniper got down before he arrived and had left. Ray decided to wait a little longer. Then a head furtively peeped over the stairway. Noting that all seemed clear, the gunman dropped from the roof to the balcony of the stairs and began his careful way down. Ray watched from cover until the man began heading towards him. Ray flattened himself against the wall just around the corner. As the man peered around the corner to make sure the way was still clear, a huge fist slammed into the surprised man's face. He was knocked backwards and fell onto his back, face bleeding profusely. Ray immediately pounced upon the unfortunate victim and 'frisked' him. A snub nosed pistol was taken from him along with a silencer which had been dissembled.

"What the ding-dong do you think you are doing?" Ray asked of Hector.

The man paled under his bloody face as he beheld his own gun pointing at his temple.

"Nuthin' personal – it was orders!" Hec said, his frightened look pleading with his intended victim.

"Who's orders? Need I ask?" Ray gritted through clenched teeth. "Why does the boss want me taken down; I never squealed!"

"He reckons he saw you with the cops when you come out of the sewage drain."

Hec regained a bit of composure now that he was not straight away shot; something he would have done himself.

"What sewage drain? The cops arrested me and took me in, I don't know of any sewage drain!" Ray asked.

"Awright, so it was a mistake – lemme up!"

"I am keeping your gun and a firm eye on you. I can see that you can not be trusted. Get in my car and you drive. We are going to see the boss and get this sorted out!" Ray ordered.

"Huh! Gee, you are taking a risk aren't you?" Hec said, awe in his voice.

"No!" Ray quietly informed. "I know he is armed but he does not know I am. If I have to – I will put him away!"

Hec just shook his head in disbelief. When they arrived at Drew Slimmery's office, Ray motioned for Hec to lead the way. He walked past the secretary who recognised them both and nodded. Hec knocked upon the door.

"Come in, I wanted to go over - ? Oh! You are not my secretary. Is the job done?" Drew Slimmery looked up from his desk and asked Hec. Then went pale as he saw the gun pointing at Hector Stroud's head. The grim-faced Ray covered by his body.

"I want some answers or you both cop it – why did you set your dog onto me? Keep your hands where I can see them!"

"But – but I thought I saw you. You're not arrested and -!!" Slimy looked like his nickname.

"I was arrested. They took me in when the bust was on. I got a good barrister. Had a word with Dermutt while I was in too!" Ray supplied.

Drew Slimmery was cautious; he hedged in indecision.

"Just hold your horses. I have a contact in the big house. No do not do anything foolish for a minute. I can easily find out!" Ignoring the fact that Ray had the gun, Drew calmly picked up his telephone. Ray and Hector waited while he made a call.

"It's me – yes – did you have a Raymond Cress inside today – yes I will hang on." There was silence for a minute, and then Drew nodded. "Ugh-huh-and what about Dermutt?" Again they waited while the message was passed on. Drew replaced the receiver, and then looked up. He smiled apologetically. "Yes, well; it seems that you were apprehended with the others and a Mister Hingiss posted bail for you. Please accept my apologies but I have to be careful." Drew was regaining his composure.

"I take acceptation to being used for target practice. If it happens again I will not bother bringing your fellows in alive!" Ray affected an air of bravado.

"Quite, I would not expect you to either. It was just a misunderstanding, it will not happen again!"

Ray snapped.

"I got into this business because I can do with the extra cash. If you are going to make life miserable for me – well I am getting out. I got rid of Johnson for you and was going to get Hewie off your back but the cops got to him first. I have proved myself but still you set your terrier on to me. Now what is it to be – am I going to be hounded or do I start clearing the floor now?" Ray gave the impression he did not care one way or the other. The gun in his hand moved from one to the other. His narrowed eyes closely watched for the slightest adverse move towards him. Carefully, so as not to aggravate the man with the weapon, Drew held a hand up palm outwards.

"All right, I am sorry; it was just a damn misunderstanding. Do not do anything foolish, we will resolve the matter right here and now!" Drew addressed Hec Stroud.

"Hec, it was a mistake. He is one of us. You two will work as a part of a team – is that understood?" Hec nodded.

"You is the Boss, whatever you say goes." He turned to Ray. "No hard feelings, I was just doing my job!" Ray looked deep into the man's eyes, then nodded. Relieved, Drew reached into his inside coat pocket and keenly watched by Ray; withdrew a wad of notes.

"I will give each of you a thousand, just to show there is no animosity; we are all in this together. Now I have been hit hard of late, not only by the 'feds' but also by that snivelling dickhead Larry –" he looked at Ray "- Hec is keeping an eye on him for us. Now because I am getting hit so much, the purse will have to be tightened until I become more solvent. While you two are here, let us get our heads together and see if we can come up with some answers." Drew addressed Hec. "Have you got any idea where he is cutting my stuff yet?" Hec shook his head.

"No, but I do know that we are going somewhere 'secret' tomorrow."

Drew paused with hand on chin, thinking.

"Sounds interesting. Will this be the first time he has used you as a bodyguard?"

Hec shook his head.

"Nah! But the other times he just went to the betting shop and then on to one of the boxer's places. This time I think it is something more important; he is worried that you might have a price on him!" Hec grinned.

"By George he needs to be worried!" Drew snarled. "We need to locate my goods and take it back, when we have it; then you may dispose of him. Make sure I get my stuff first!" Drew demanded.

"Yes Boss!"

"Have you got any plans to get more goodies?" Ray asked, as if he was passing the time of day. Drew was about to retort aggressively when he remembered that this man was not just a hired thug. He tactfully answered.

"When the next delivery is to be serviced I will contact you; meanwhile we have to replace some staff. Any one got any ideas; my latest recruit was working for the opposition!" He waited, giving the two in his confidence time to think.

"Well, there is Gerry –" Ray began. Drew cut him off.

"Ah yes, your second-in-command at the warehouse. Dermutt spoke of him. Can he be trusted?"

"When I am not there Gerry is as good as me!" Ray replied.

"That sounds good enough for me. If this 'Gerry' is anywhere like the man you are he could be a worthwhile acquisition." Drew smiled, and then added. "Unfortunately I do not have goods to be worked at present.

"Gerry has taken his cut all the way through, so he is already on your payroll"

"Mmm, yes, that is so – I had forgotten about him, I left that part of it to Dermutt. Okay, he is one; any others?" Drew looked hopefully at Hec.

"No, not from me, I have just arrived from interstate. I don't know anybody yet!"

"Well it is a worry; still, I will get more trusted men. Money talks and it should not be hard to replace them, in the meantime Ray, you and Gerry will have to do the filling in; are you okay with that?"

"Yes mister Slimmery."

"Right, well now I have another problem at the moment and that is my Asian connection. I do not know just how much they know of my affairs as yet, but you can be sure that they are well-informed and sooner or later I will be accosted by them about Dermutt. If either of you two is approached about Dermutt, just tell it as you know it – he has been put away but I have a better replacement. That is all you tell them. The Asian connection paid me a visit and I have to be aware that nothing more goes wrong, or else I will have them on my back too. You two get back to your posts and when next I need you – or in the event Larry lets something slip – I shall contact you! Dismissed." He waved them out. Ray made sure that Hec was well on his way to Larry Crumpers Gymnasium before he made his secretive way to see Lieutenant Jason Ferguson. That he was not followed was ensured by his getting a taxi cab and instructing the driver to go in a round-about way to get there. Quickly entering the premises, Ray hurried to Jason's quarters.

"Good grief!" Detective Sergeant Carey exclaimed upon seeing the giant form in their office. "Wet the bed. To what do we owe for the pleasure of this visit?"

Ray smiled and motioned for Graeme to come and be privy to what he had to offer Jason. They waited expectantly. Ray informed the two of what had happened since his release from prison. Finishing with –

"- and so now that I have cemented my position within the cartel and beaten off 'hit man' Hec Stroud, I am going to get Gerry more involved within the cartel too!" "Phew! You do not muck about do you? Now it is imperative that we close the book on this cartel quickly. They are weakened at the moment and very vulnerable, we must catch Drew with the goods and if at all possible; the Asian connection too!" Jason re-affirmed the obvious.

"Slimmery mentioned another cartel; somehow they have been getting Drew's deliveries. What do you know about them?" Ray asked.

"It is just a stand-over guy who hates Drew's guts. Not really a cartel; still a force to be closed down. He is just an opportunist who runs a gymnasium and has a few prize fighters on his payroll. Fixes fights and makes a lot of money out of it, the trouble is that the average gambler is taken for a sucker. We want to close him down too but so far, we have not been able to pin anything on him!" Graeme supplied.

"If we could somehow manage to catch the two of them with something illegal, boy, wouldn't that be something." Jason frowned.

"Believe it or not but that just may be a possibility!" Ray informed the two surprised detectives. Both looked to Ray expectantly, waiting for him to elaborate.

"Slimy is incensed that his hated enemy has taken him down for a shipment or two and he has his own 'spy' planted in Larry's employ. Now I know for a fact that an execution is planned for Larry, as soon

as Hec finds out where Larry is trying to 'cut' his stolen goods."
Jason cut him short.

"So Hec is on Larry's payroll but in reality he is working for Slimmery?"

"Correct!" Ray informed.

"Now if I can manage to have Slimmery watch the supposed demise of Larry when Hec has located the missing drugs; we may be able to pin them both at the one time!"

He sat back with a Cheshire cat grin beaming from his face.

"That would be great but most improbable. From what I can see, this here damned Slimmery is as slippery as an eel!" Jason thoughtfully said.

"Still, there is a slight hope; is there not?" Graeme, forever the optimist suggested.

"Yes, I will see what I can arrange. Being privy to the high bloke in the cartel should help!" Ray solemnly stated.

CHAPTER SIXTEEN

Ray was back at the office of Drew Slimmery.

"Are you still going ahead with this here attack on Larry Crumpers?" He blatantly asked.

"Oh, what do you know of that?" Drew keenly appraised his second-in-command.

"It is just that Hec and I were going over what we had to do, we have to be co-ordinated. And it was mentioned that Thursday in the morning you have a 'surprise' cooked up for Crumpers; but I thought you had to locate your stolen 'stuff' first?" Ray frowned.

"Ah yes, glad you are on the ball. I must ring through and cancel that; it will be on hold until I have secured that shipment. Excuse me a minute while I 'phone my connections!" Drew did so. Then turned to Ray.

"Look, I made a mistake about you; I could have sworn that you were amongst the officers who tried to detain me when the Richmond Plant was raided again. I actually saw a couple of huge fellows that could have been you."

"Most coppers are big blokes." Ray defended.

"Yes, quite. Well, so I was mistaken. Now I have a most important job for you to do. I need for you to be coerced into working for Larry Crumpers!"

"What?" Ray showed his surprise. "What brought that on?"

"Hec has been asked if he knows a good bloke to get on-side. At first he did not know anyone but after considering it, he suggested to Larry that you were ripe for the picking if you got more than I pay you. Since Dermutt got lumbered, you are supposed to be at a loose end. Hec said he would sound you out. Now I need for you to be on his payroll so that we can feed him some false information. Maybe then we can get him out of the way while I make a devastating raid on the poor fool he has 'cutting' my goods. It is imperative that I get it back – are you up to it?" Drew gazed at Ray through keen slitted eyes, daring Ray to back off. Ray did not let him down.

"On my terms. See, I am supposed to be a warehouse foreman. But working for you and now if I get this job you want that I should; hell, I am going to be flat out!"

He had a firm set to his jaw as he stood up to this undoubted rogue.

"It should only be for a little while – 'til I get my goods back – then we may have the problem of Larry Crumpers finalized, permanently!"

Drew had a wicked gleam in his eyes.

"Okay, but Hec still takes orders from me."

"Sure, sure, you will only be guided by his suggestions. You will have complete control. Drew smiled; oilily.

Hec Stroud was waiting by Ray's car when the big men had knocked off for the day.

"The boss said not to interfere with your work load, so I waited for you to finish." Hec sheepishly offered.

"I take it that I have to meet this 'Larry' of yours!"

"Yeah. Get in your car and follow me!"

Hec said, a little bravado showing. Ray let it slip and followed. They convoyed but a matter of four kilometres when Hector pulled into the kerb of a seedy little back street in North Melbourne.

"This is his Gym; they need to search you for weapons. Are you 'heeled'?" Hec asked.

"I am only armed when I need to be!" Ray offered a little bravado himself.

A flap inside the door opened and a face which unmistakeably belonged to a 'pug', peered out. When he recognised Hec, the door was opened.

"Oo's ya mate?"

"Larry has ordered him here!" Hec pushed past.

The bruiser put a restraining hand upon Ray's shoulder.

"Hand's off!" Ray quickly brushed him aside and faced the man.

"Hey, go easy damn ya. He's only doin' his job. Ya gotta let him search ya!"

"No one puts a hand on me!" Ray was defiant.

"Aw, for cris' sake let him pat you down!" Hec argued. Ray held his arms out.

"I am not armed" He quietly said as the bruiser lightly patted him down.

"Okay!" Ray was allowed to proceed.

"So, you work for Dermutt?" Larry asked.

"The cops got him." Ray nodded.

"Hec seems to think that you might be willing to switch camps if the price is right?" Larry persisted.

"Could be – they seem to bumble things a bit! I'm listening." Ray affected his 'devil-may-care' attitude.

"Slimmery and me do not get on too well. What is he paying you?" Larry hedged.

"Not enough. Make a worthwhile offer and I just may be coaxed!" Ray sneered. "I intend to run the smart-arse into the ground, but to do it I need to know when and where his shipments are due. I can give you cash money – no questions asked – if you decide to back me. Are you in the know about his shipments?"

Larry watched his latest employee with shrewd eyes; the eyes that could determine when a fighter was willing to throw in the towel.

"I am only new at this caper. He has not confided in me yet. But, if you can show me how genuine you are, well, maybe as soon as I find out I can let Hec know – he can pass it on to you. How is that?" Ray raised his eyebrows in query.

"So long as we have time to intercept the stuff; sounds all right to me.

Larry went to his safe next door and returned with a bundle of notes.

"Here, that is a thousand to show I am serious and you get another lot when you have some news for me!"

Ray left Hec and Larry in the gymnasium and returned to his home.

The very next day at around eleven in the morning, Hec again fronted his boss.

"Now you are positive this address is the one my goods are languishing at?"

Drew eagerly checked with Hector, just to re-affirm himself.

"Sure is Boss. I saw the joker working on it and he reckons that a good swag of it will be ready later today!" Hec grinned.

"Well now, I must ring my man back and tell him to get the surprise ready for Larry. He may not come if we set the 'delivery' for Saturday evening, so I will arrange it for two o'clock on Sunday morning. See that Larry knows that I am personally going to supervise its delivery because too much of my stuff is going missing. That should ensure that he comes himself, the stuffy little shit will want to witness my downfall!"

"As good as done, Boss!" Hec smiled as he left with his deadly message.

The raid on Larry's 'cutting' room was quick, efficient and deadly. Silas Gronin whom Drew got to replace Vernon Chamberlain, in his own distribution and cutting rooms; had two seedy side-kicks who were not much on brains but deadly as assassins. These two were sent to 'get rid' of anyone who stood in their way when they raided Larry's 'cutting' room. To get his goods back, Drew ordered that the sky was the limit; therefore Larry's 'cutter' and his assistant were unceremoniously slaughtered when the raid took place. Drew got his merchandise then went all out for Larry. Hec saw to it that Larry was made aware that Drew was responsible for the raid and that he had a bigger shipment of drugs coming in at two on Sunday morning, as reported to him by Ray. Larry was as mad as a meat-axe and ordered that Hec accompanied him on a 'get even' mission. Larry was going to hit hard at Drew where he would feel it most – his hip pocket! Therefore at ten to two on Sunday morning, they were at the air-strip, hidden and awaiting the shipment's arrival. Drew Slimmery was all agog with excitement when he was told by Hec that his arch enemy Larry had fallen for his trap. Drew had Ray accompany him as a bodyguard and the two of them awaited the arrival of Larry's vehicle at a vantage point some ten kilometres from the airstrip. Ray was not aware of the reason for Drew's need of him as a bodyguard. The distant drone of an aircraft was heard by the pair as they waited.

"Ah, there comes the plane now!" Drew smiled.

"Huh! What plane?" Ray asked.

"Delivering my goods!" Was the unanswered question. "We will have to wait while it is unloaded and then reloaded into Larry's waiting car!"

"Larry's?" Ray asked, questioningly.

"Oh yes!" Drew gave a sickly smile.

Ray was doing some quick thinking. What should he do? Evidently a trap had been primed for Larry, but what sort of trap. Perhaps the plane was full of gunmen and a slaughter was devised. If so, why would Drew be waiting ten miles from the action. One would think that as Drew had set it up, he would want to witness the downfall of his rival? Ray was pondering whether he should arrest Drew now and try to stop the bloodshed, but then, he could not just arrest him without proof. That was counter productive! Then a motor cars headlights could be seen approaching. Drew Slimmery had his head and shoulders out of the side window watching the approaching vehicle, an expectant look on his features.

"Anytime now." He muttered.

Ray was at his wits end with questions, when suddenly it happened. The approaching vehicle disappeared amidst a blinding flash, followed a few seconds later by a tremendous boom as the car exploded and disintegrated.

"Good grief!" Ray exclaimed. "We had better get over there and see if there are any survivors!"

"There won't be!" Drew smiled grimly. "I had them put in a charge big enough to destroy the lot!" Ray looked with derision at Drew.

"You – you had the car booby-trapped?" Drew glanced very smugly at his bodyguard.

"No, not booby-trapped. But my case of goods that they were trying to steal was, and they fell for it!" Ray looked incredulously at his 'boss'.

"Hector may have been in that blast!"

"No, I do not think so. He was told to get rid of the pilot. He should be safe in the aircraft!"

Ray shook his head in amazement. He would have something to report to Jason now.

When the aircraft touched down, Larry and Hec, with the two bruisers, approached it. Surprised that Drew's mob was not there, they went ahead and boarded the aircraft. Hec held the pilot at gunpoint while the two bruisers unloaded and put the supposed contraband in their vehicle. Surprised that Drew had not put in an appearance, Larry ordered that they scoot before he did. Hec was still holding the pilot at gunpoint when the pilot 'gunned' the plane and the aircraft shot forwards tipping Hec off balance. The aircraft taxied off quickly and headed for the skies. Larry set his vehicle in motion and scurried away before Drew and his mob appeared.

"They have took Hec!" One of the bruisers said.

"Yeah!" Larry worried. "Ah, Hec can take care of himself. He will probably be back before we will." Was the callous reply.

Meanwhile, in the aircraft, Hec and the pilot were having a laugh.

"Let us circle around and witness the big boom!" Hec suggested.

"Yair. I am all for that – gee I was worried when I had that parcel – what if it wasn't timed right!" The pilot breathed a sigh of relief.

They sighted the headlights seconds before they disappeared in the huge explosion.

"Ah well, you can drop me off back in town and I will get a taxi back to the boss's place. He will not mind paying for it now!" Hec grinned.

Back at his office, Drew was talking with his East-side distributor. "Well you did a good job of recovery of my goods and we now have Larry's mob off our backs. Here is your payments for a job well done; see that you pay off the rest of the money due to your accomplices. When the goods are ready I will have Ray disperse it to our other outlets and then maybe we can get a long-delayed shipment of weapons to our buyer. There is another mob up in the hills who may be interested too, now that Larry is no more with us. They may be ripe for the picking. I will see if I can have Ray locate this 'secret army'; dismissed!"

Ray too, was back at the office but this was Jason's office. "Slippery does not do the man justice, nor does Slimy. This man has got to be stopped!" Jason thumped a huge fist into his other palm. "Let us put relevant known data together and see can we pin him down. Ray, beginning with the apprehension of Dermutt; go over once again what you know!" Jason ordered.

"All right. Now let me see. Dermutt got arrested and I had to have an excuse for not being taken down with him. I managed to talk my way out of that by being 'clean', no money and no drugs on me; I managed to put that over Slimmery. Then I allowed myself to be coerced into taking a higher profile in the cartel, thanks to Dermutt being out of it. I delivered a good swag of contraband to 'Fatty' and we managed to swing a 'bust' on him. Meantime Drew had me pick up a load for him and we tried to implicate him. He outsmarted us through that damned secret tunnel he had built into the building. As an alibi for me but also to try and bleed Dermutt; I was imprisoned with him. He let nothing slip but it concreted my alibi, because Drew saw me and set Hec Stroud to kill me. That misfired because of a lucky note I found at my car when he took a pot shot at me!"

"You did not tell us about that!" Jason cut in.

"I didn't think finding the note was important." Ray answered.

"Everything is important!" Jason stressed. "Go on!"

"Well, I zigzagged my car over to where the shot came from- !"

"That is the second shot." Graeme supplied.

"See, that is what I mean – every detail!" Jason urged.

Ray looked hard and long at his superior officer.

"Yes Sir. I stopped the car out of sight under the awning of the factory where Hec was hiding and waited for fifteen minutes; in silence. Hector must have thought that I sped off because he did not seem to expect me to stay. When he came down the back stairs and peeped around the corner to see if the way was clear; that is when I punched and disarmed him. I took him back to Drew and demanded an apology because I was arrested and in the clink with the rest of the men arrested at the Richmond factory."

"What did Drew have to say about that?" Jason asked, although he knew as Ray had already told him.

"Seeing that I had a gun pointing at him and being behind Hec, he had to soothe me down a bit. Well then he rang someone – I don't know who – but I believe it was a warden 'inside', and he was told that I was in there but had been released by my Barrister turning up. A mister Hingiss, I have never heard of him –"

"He is the police special crimes barrister; we have him cover this sort of thing." Jason supplied.

"- right; well he did his job well. Then Drew called a truce amongst us and told Hec that sicking him onto me was a mistake. So we had to kiss and make up. Then we began plotting the next move."

"And?" Jason asked.

"Well it was suggested I work for Larry Crumpers because he asked Hec if he knew anyone in the cartel who may know some of Drew's secrets. Hec nominated me and took me to meet Larry. Hec told Larry about Drew's next shipment and said he got it from me – I actually had nothing to do with it – but it now appears that it was the deadly 'set-up' that killed Larry!" Ray paused to catch his breath.

"So now Drew is in the clear so far as someone thieving his shipments is concerned. I wonder if he might try to take over some of Larry's contacts." Jason surmised.

"Like who?" Graeme wanted to know.

"Oh I do not know – Larry must have had someone in mind to pass the drugs on to!" Jason worried.

"What about that rogue army up in the hills where Colin and Evan got nabbed?" Graeme put in.

"Yes, them for instance. We must try harder to find them. I will ring the local Sergeant up there and see if they have anything for us!" Jason considered.

"I am pretty sure that is not who he had in mind for the drugs though; the guns yes. Now, is that all Ray?"

"Except that Drew will want to brief me on his next move tomorrow!"

"Right, well let us know what that brings."

CHAPTER SEVENTEEN

When Ray had left to return to his workplace at the warehouse, Jason and Graeme got their heads together to try and find a chink in the armour of the cartel.

"Now the scene of the explosion that killed Larry is being investigated by the forensic department; that may determine who were the victims and the type of explosives used but I doubt that it will prove who authorised it. We know that Slimmery organised it and the fact that he witnessed the demise of Larry by being at the scene with one of our people in the wee small hours of the morning, gives credence to the fact of him being a major contributor to Larry's death; but at the moment, leaves us without actual proof of his involvement. We have to somehow tie him in with this brutal slaying. Sure, he got Larry off our backs and maybe stopped a booming business in drugs and contraband weapons taking effect; but Larry was only a piker. The illegal 'army' is still to be apprehended as too, does Slimmery's contacts who dispose of drugs and illicit side-arms and ouzi assault rifles. Goodness knows what else he may have brought into the country!" Jason worried.

"Possibly rocket launchers and the likes for all we know!" Graeme supplied.

"Well there is no proof of those weapons as yet but yes, anything is possible!" Jason agreed.

"What about the Asian connection?" Graeme asked.

"That is a worry. We may have to rely on our international connections to control them. If we supply all relevant information, I believe they can handle that. Our main concern is to stamp out the growth of this stranglehold that the cartels have in our own backyard!" Jason was determined that he would do his best with the current problem. "I am relying heavily upon two men who are not trained in counter- espionage but are so far, doing a magnificent job!"

Hec Stroud was back at Drew Slimmery's office.

"Ah, how did you go – have no trouble with Johannas?" The slimy one asked.

"Piece of cake. Nearly broke my neck when he 'gunned' the engine though. I did a back-flip down the fuselage when he shot off. We circled around and watched from the sky – geez – what a sight. There ain't much left of Larry's auto!"

"Yes, beautiful. I watched from a vantage point too. That will teach the hound to pilfer my stock. Now here is your 'cut' and I have an envelope here that I want you to give Johannas personally; it is his stipend for carrying the 'parcel'. It was dangerous and he certainly earned it. Now that you don't have to bother with Larry anymore, it will give you something to do. I must keep Johannas onside seeing that we have lost Hewie. He still must be dealt with but I will have that done from 'inside'."

Hec grinned as he accepted the envelope and went about doing as was ordered.

Detective Jim Lynton, the intelligence telephone operator, took the tape of the conversation he just heard straight away to Jason, after having his assistant monitor the departure of Hec Stroud from Slimmery's office.

"Well done Jim!" Jason applauded upon hearing that immediate action was taken.

"We should be able to locate the aircraft that delivered the bomb and its pilot now!"

Agent Riley had picked up his partner Frank; together they 'tailed' Hec at a discreet distance. Their journey took them to the intermediate aerodrome just on the outskirts of the main metropolis proper. Hec went directly to the hangar that housed the small passenger aircraft that was used in the delivery of the explosive parcel. After fifteen minutes, Hec returned to his vehicle and the detectives let him go about his business. Hec was unaware that he had been 'tailed' to the airport. The pilot, Johannas, still had the envelope of money he had been given by Hec; including fingerprints. It was carefully confiscated and Johannas was arrested on suspicion and his aircraft grounded for inspection by the forensic crew. When undercover agents Max Riley and Frank Dean reported to Jason, he was suitably impressed by their work.

"So you say that Johannas still had the envelope that the money came in?" Jason queried.

"Yes Jason, he had opened it to count the money I suppose but then put it back; lucky for us!" Detective Riley acknowledged.

"Right, I only hope that forensic finds all three sets of prints on it. This could be the break-through we have been waiting for!" Jason smiled hugely. "Have you arranged for the plane to be scrutinised?"

"Yes, I rang through after we arrested Johannas."

"Good!"

"That may tie Slimmery to the payment but it does nothing to prove that he was involved with the bombing!" Graeme said.

"Unless we can get Johannas to talk!" Jason thoughtfully rested his chin in his fingers.

Once again Ray had cause to urgently see Drew Slimmery. He took time off from work

"Gerry got a message that the boss of the toy factory wished to see me?" Ray said, with raised eyebrows.

"Yes. Sorry that I had to interrupt you at work. There was no other way to get in touch before you went home. Silas has a batch of goodies ready for distribution at the East Side. I need for you to go and pick up the stuff then get it to - !! Oh, excuse me."

Drew answered his telephone. Ray watched as Drew's face went through a series of expressions.

"When. It is in progress now?" The face of his boss visible paled. "Damn their interfering hides!" Drew slammed the receiver down and turned to Ray. "My bloody East Side cutting and distributing rooms are being raided right now. I do not know if or how many of my men are apprehended. Bugger the bloody 'feds', I wish they would mind their own blasted business. I am getting slowly forced out of business. Hell! If the Asian boys hear of this I could be in dire trouble!"

Inwardly Ray was quite elated. He gave no outward sign.

"Gee, you could have sent me head first into a trap!" He grizzled.

Drew sharply looked at him, and then snapped.

"Well I didn't. Shut up a minute; I got to think!" He cogitated for a few minutes, and then retrieved his telephone. "You had better get down to the station and see what can be saved of Silas Gronin's crew. Yes, they have just raided my East Side factory. I do not know – everything I suppose – I am running out of patience with this 'leak'. Okay report back when you have something to tell me!!"

Drew again replaced the receiver, this time a little more sedately. He turned to Ray.

"You just lost a job. I will call again when you are needed, dismissed."

With a peremptory wave of his hand, Ray was given the boot.

"Strike me, no wonder Dermutt was getting uptight with him!"

Ray mused to himself as he quit the building.

Graeme Carey went into his superior's office.

"I just got a call from that country station near where the ouzi's were being used."

He told Jason.

"And?" His boss asked.

"It appears that the 'silent' army has heard that it is being sought out over it's shipment of firearms, and they purposely let a 'leak' come into the local station to leave a telephone number there. Evidently they want the law off their backs and they thought that by providing the contact number, we would be satisfied to track down the source of the contraband; therefore leaving them alone!"

"Interesting." Jason said. "And have you got the boys working on the number yet?" Graeme shook his head.

"No, not yet. I have only just this minute received the call from them. Shall I push it through?"

"Ugh – huh, by the way, summon Detective Murphy to come and see me will you – urgently?" Jason went back to shuffling through his papers.

Shortly thereafter, Eugene Murphy made his appearance.

"You summoned me here Sir?"

"Oh yes, Eugene. Look, I think that you had best get an assistant to help you with those two at the warehouse. Things are coming to a head and although all is comparatively quiet at the moment; all hell could bust loose at any time now!" Jason peered at his man. "I believe that Slimmery is getting close to breaking point and he could lash out at the nearest person to him. Ray may very well be that person. He is becoming far too involved for my liking but only he can do the work at present. I want that you keep a very wary eye upon your two responsibilities and do not let up; that is when a slip can be expected. Do you follow?" Jason wanted no risks taken with his two plants in the cartel.

"Yes Sir. I will organise another agent immediately Sir!" With a smart salute, he left.

Meanwhile Ray and Gerry were discussing the cartel in private.

"And what is it like to be privy to the big man himself?" Gerry asked.

"I will be glad when it is over. This slippery character is like a bucketful of his namesakes. Slimy eels! He can be real mean by the looks of him. I have had to play it as though I do not care one way or the other with him, I tell you though, he can fly off the handle if things do not go the way he plans them. Only by being a strong type can I manage him. He wears a hidden gun at the back, I noticed it the other day when he went to a cupboard; you could see it bulge out when he bent down to pick up a paper from the floor. It is a wonder he has not shot himself in the leg or the buttocks. We have him worried because he has lost a lot of shipments. Things must be getting tough for him – and he has his Asian connection on his back, due to all the arrests and then Larry getting in on the act!" Ray grinned.

"Serves the lanky lout right, he must have brought lots of misery onto many different people through his drug imports; and for what? Just money – heaps of it by all accounts!" Gerry showed his contempt for the man.

"The main thing at the moment is to try and get him implicated into this filthy demise of his opposite number, Larry. I was there at the scene of the dastardly deed, but could do nothing to prevent it – I did not even know that it was about to happen – couldn't have done anything even if I did know. The scoundrel has to be tied in with it, we know he ordered the bombing but knowing and proving; are two different things!" Ray gave a wry grin. "Pity he was not a bit closer to the action, I might have been able to get him involved somehow!"

"By all accounts, he is too cunning to let himself get mixed up in any covert action himself; look after number one appears to be his motto." Gerry advised.

"You are not wrong. He seems to let every one else take the risks while he remains in the clear, we have to reverse that by crikey!" Ray murmured a firm set to his jaw.

Carl Schliffler had been interrogated at some length but had failed to let anything slip. He was a Drew Slimmery man through and through. After all, Carl knew how his boss could fly off the handle at the drop of a hat; albeit in the privacy of his office. Outside, he held himself in remarkably well. Carl was let go as a free man after he was interviewed and the raid on the Richmond plant was conducted. That plant was closed down when the undeniable proof of the illicit drugs found at the premises had been acknowledged. Of course, Carl knew nothing of the drugs but never-the-less; shut down the premises were! It was because he had no business to attend that he went to see what Drew wanted him to do now. Drew was not at all the smug, self centred man of the weeks before. Now he had the weight of knowing the Asian connection would be monitoring his every move. His own life was in danger. Carl almost crept in when he came to see what his boss needed for him to do now, after being primed of Drew's apparently uncertain state, by the man's secretary.

"Why were you not at the factory like I ordered you to be?" Were the first words abruptly put to him? Carl stammered.

"But Boss, I was arrested in the early hours before the shipment was delivered!"

Drew looked at the cowering man steadily.

"What made the curs arrest you – especially at that time of the morning? You must have given them some cause for it?"

"N – No Boss. I never did nothin', I had only just arrived and they pounced on me. They must have been tipped off or something – it was not my fault!" Drew scowled at his man who had charge of the Richmond Plant.

"Something stinks there!" He said, and then changed the subject.

"Any idea what has happened to Johannas? He has not answered his 'phone for two days!" Drew asked of Carl.

"Huh? No, I don't have much to do with him, is he up at the aerodrome or maybe at the airstrip?" The man puzzled.

"No, I have checked all his usual haunts. No one has seen hide or hair of him lately. I must contact him soon, as the exporters are giving me a rough time of it with expected deliveries. I have to verify that we will be on hand to receive the cargoes!"

Drew thumped his desk in anger.

"Why in blazes is everything going amiss lately? And another thing; there still seems to be a leak in the organization!"

"Yeah. I do not know how the 'feds' happened to take me in and leave the way clear to jump the shipment at Richmond!" Carl snarled.

"They did not only raid the place, they nearly captured me as well. I thought at first that Ray was involved; I could have sworn I saw him come out of the sewer after I got clear. But he was in custody, so that sort of cleared him. Just as well, he has done Dermutt's work okay but still we get bagged; it is as if they have a glass on everything we do!" Drew worried. "Are you absolutely certain that your own telephone is in the clear?" Carl had the temerity to ask. Drew gave him a withering look, and then frowned.

"Perhaps I should check with my technician!"

At headquarters for the squad that arrested the pilot who received the quite large envelope of cash, Detective Riley had cause to speak on the telephone to his superior.

"Jason, it is Max Riley here."

"Yes, what do you have?"

"Got Johannas to let something slip, he is not aware of it – it just came out." Max went on to explain. "During questioning we asked him what about his last delivery, who was it for. I explained that it was damning evidence against him. He blurted that he could not be held responsible for someone else's property. If it exploded after he delivered it, which was not his fault."

"Oh. I take it you never mentioned that it was an explosive package?" Jason smiled as he asked.

"No, he put his foot in it there, shall we hold him?" Max enquired with tongue in cheek.

"Ha, yes hold him, I think that he may let more slip if we give him some time to cogitate; I may come over. Good work Max."

In a matter of only an hour, Jason was in the rooms occupied by the detectives given the job of grilling Johannas. He joined with Frank Dean who was the partner of Max and continued the interview with a worried Johannas. Jason replayed the tape of his previous interview. When the part in which Johannas could be clearly expressing that – 'if it exploded after he delivered it that was not his fault' – was aired; Jason stopped the tape.

"Well, what do you have to add to that Johannas?" He asked.

Johannas after listening to what he had said paled and badly tried to square himself.

"How did you know that the package you carried would explode, killing three men? You understand that you are now the prime suspect for murder?"

Jason grimly outlined to the downhearted pilot.

"But I only had the job of carrying the damned parcel; I didn't prime it or sent it!" Johannas pleaded.

"As far as we know you brought the bomb that killed three men, therefore unless we know otherwise; you will stand trial for their murder!" Jason rose to go. "Think it over. Are you going to take the rap for someone else?"

CHAPTER EIGHTEEN

"You wanted to see me?" Carl Schiffler asked of Drew when he was summoned.

"Yes Carl, we are depleted of staff a little at the moment. I have had my Richmond and East Side places closed down and many good men are apprehended, therefore I really need a trusted man to consummate the distribution of 'hard stuff' at Moorabbin. It has been raided and at the moment the 'feds' seem to have by-passed the Toy Factory. What I need from you is to quietly set a small corner of the factory to work 'cutting' a new batch that has been ordered in. I am going to have it put through the customs warehouse now that my aircraft means has been thwarted. Ray is in charge there and I see no reason why the goods will not get through. Can I rely on you?"

Drew sincerely hoped that this time things would go right for him. After all, that snivelling hound Larry was now out of his hair and with Hewie behind the wall and Johannas disappeared; he had to resort to whatever means he had available. Thank his lucky stars that two dependable people like Carl and Ray were still around! Hec Stroud was ordered to be on hand to pick up the shipment and to deliver it to the Moorabbin Factory when Ray notified Drew it was ready. A week had passed before the goods were in the warehouse.

Ray dutifully notified Jason of its presence and he arranged for the flying squad to replace the drugs with flour. The next morning Drew was told to arrange delivery of his crate that by now had a 'bug' securely hidden. Hec turned up and was given the crate by Gerry.

"Here we go again!" Gerry jubilantly noted. Ray just smiled.

"A good effort has been put into tracing this lot. I only hope all is in order!"

Carl Schiffler accepted the goods off Hec and asked him to help get the crate into the back part of the factory where Carl had set up his workshop.

"Better make sure it is the good stuff; help me with this lid Hec!"

Carl asked the gunman.

"Oh, lovely!" Carl tasted a bit on the end of his finger; then spat it out. "Shit!" He exclaimed. "This is flour!"

"Hell!" Cried Hec, racing for all he was worth to his van. It was then that the squad moved in and arrested Carl, but Hec, already on the run, eluded them. He was unable to make his way to the van and stole a passing vehicle from a workman who was in the act of locking it after having just arrived. With a gun waved in his face the man stood still and let the madman with the gun have his way. Hec careened off, weaving in and out among the agents who were pursuing him. He made a clean getaway! At Drew Slimmery's office, he was on the telephone and his pallid face paled even more as he heard Hec describing what had happened.

"There is only one answer and that is to stop this 'leak' permanently. Go immediately to the warehouse and eliminate Ray!"

"What! But you said you made a mistake – he was one of us?" Hec puzzled.

"It is quite evident now that Ray has been the leak all along. This man is number one traitor and you will not mess up this time. If you do – well, just do him in permanently. That is an order!"

"Yes Boss. He is as good as dead!"

Hec hung up the telephone and with a very grim look, began his manhunt.

Detective Lynton the telephone operator who was monitoring all of Drew Slimmery's calls, immediately rang Jason to tell him of the urgent intercept just made. Everyone moved into action. Hec Stroud entered the warehouse and made his way through the security doors. The alarms went off when his firearm was detected. Hec ignored the alarm and made his way to where Gerry and Ray were going over some paperwork. He drew his pistol and calmly aimed it at Ray.

"Freeze – Police!" He was ordered.

The warning came just in time for Ray and Gerry to duck behind a crate as bullets whistled about. Hec, having missed because of the warning, calmly turned and aimed his pistol at the approaching officers. He was cut down in a hail of fire from the two officers whose job it was to protect the foreman and his assistant.

"Crikey!" Ray exclaimed. "That was close!"

"I'll say!" Gerry acknowledged.

"It would appear that your cover has been blown!" Detective Eugene Murphy stated.

"Sooner or later it had to happen!" Ray agreed.

Drew Slimmery was reading the newspaper early on the following day. A report of a 'crazed' gunman being shot dead by customs officers in a blatantly brutal attack on two unarmed staff was reported. Drew was apoplectic; his rage knew no bounds as he trashed his office in a frenzied attack to relieve his feelings. His secretary – bodyguard, quite used to these outbursts, tried desperately to calm his beleaguered boss.

"Do you want that I should go and finish the job Boss?" He calmly asked.

Drew, pulling himself together, stood eying the man for a time; then, calmed, replied.

"No – this bastard I will take very great pleasure in dealing with personally!"

His grim look of determination bode ill for the large foreman.

Cindy had finished the shopping and was on her way to see Natalie. The two of them had arranged to have a quiet cuppa at Natalie's home after the shopping was done. As Cindy was preparing to climb into her car, a smart little sports automobile pulled up in front of her vehicle, effectively halting its further progress.

"Oh. Excuse me; I was just about to leave. Could you let me have a little room please?"

Cindy smiled at the rather tall, thin gentleman with the expensive 'Italian cut' suit, who alighted from the sports car. The man came quite close to her and asked her name. Cindy supplied it and was administered a back-hander from the stranger. As Cindy reeled from the blow she was forcibly pushed into his sports car and the door locked on the passenger side. A gun was pointed at her and she was ordered to sit quietly and make no struggle or her husband was dead! Cindy paled and did as bidden. She was whisked away to a secret house in the country. Agent Wilbur Fox, who had been assigned to watch out for Cindy very discreetly; saw the abduction take place but was unable to get to Cindy's assistance before the sports car sped off. Unaware that the smart man in the very distinctive suit would do such a thing took him by surprise. The action took but seconds and they were gone before the undercover agent could get himself involved. He scrambled into his vehicle and took off in pursuit, frantically ringing Headquarters at the same time. Although he managed to read the numberplate of the car as it passed, he was unable to keep up with the fast little sports vehicle. Ray was answering his telephone at the time when agent Eugene Murphy urgently rushed in to inform him of the abduction. As he tried to butt in, Ray held up a hand for silence and his worried face gave Eugene to know the call was important. He overheard a little of the conversation.

"Look, don't harm her. I will come immediately. Where – no, there will be no police involved, I will be alone. Just don't hurt her. If I find that she has been harmed in any way – you will wish you were killed with Larry!"

The person on the other end could be heard to slam the receiver down, even by Eugene.

"Looks bad, I was about to tell you. Wilbur saw the abduction but was outfoxed by his nippy little sports model. Better that I rush you to see Jason!"

"No, I do not have time - !" Ray snapped.

Detective Fox was so insistent that Ray eventually said.

"Oh alright, but I need to get to Cindy. Every minute he holds her is a nightmare!"

"Do not worry overly on that score. He will not harm her until he gets his hands on you. Jason will have a plan of action mapped out. This situation has been expected – trust us!" Ray gave Eugene a frowning look.

A grim faced Jason tried to placate Ray at the Headquarters of the squad.

"Look, we have contingency plans to cover this situation – it will turn out alright – you will see!"

"That is easy for you to say, it is not your wife at risk. What happened to that 'blanket' cover you promised?" Ray snarled.

"It was in place, it is just that his sports car was too nippy for our modern cars. It will only take a few minutes to get you ready!" Ray succumbed to the police wishes.

At the farm where Cindy was being held to ransom, Drew Slimmery watched carefully as a single vehicle came up the driveway amid a cloud of dust. No other cars were in sight. The farm was isolated and stood alone in a grove of trees. There was no other building within a couple of hundred metres. Ray stopped his vehicle and sat quietly, looking for a trap. Drew watched just as expectantly from the farmhouse window. All remained static. No other person seemed to be in sight or approaching.

"Well, get out and come forward!" Drew yelled from the house.

"Let me see that my wife is safe first!" Ray called back. There was a moment's pause, and then Cindy appeared in the window. She called to ray.

"I am okay Ray; it is no use both of us dying. He cannot be trusted!"

She calmly claimed.

Drew was seen to slap her to the floor and in the interim Ray bounded from the concealment of his car and raced to the house.

He had too great a distance to cover before Drew swung back to the window. As he made his belated way to the house, a pistol shot was heard behind him and the Detective who was hidden in the boot of the car and emerged at the same time that Ray made his charge, fired at the trees surrounding the house. A sniper fell to the ground as Drew blazed away at the huge bulk of Ray. He fell to the ground. As Ray fell, a squad of agents creeping up behind the house invaded it as Drew Slimmery went to check his kill. He was just about to put a bullet in Ray's skull when the squad burst through the front door yelling out to Drew to drop his weapon. With his face twisted in rage the tall drug dealer was about to fire but thought better of it with half a dozen guns trained on him. He dropped his weapon and waited as the squad frisked him for any more weapons and took him in charge. Jason approached the body of Ray as a tearful Cindy, having had her bonds released, went to her inert husband. Jason was attending Ray and helped him to his feet.

"God Jason, get this damned vest off, it is killing me!"

Jason did so and the bullet proof vest was removed. Three bullets had hit it directly where his heart was covered.

"You would have been dead if you had not listened to us!" Jason stated the obvious.

When it was seen that his bullets had been ineffective against the bullet proof vest, Drew went into a fit of rage and but for the handcuffs, may very well have caused quite a lot of trouble.

"Not only will you be charged with kidnapping a lady but you will also be charged with the execution of one Larry Crumpers and his two thugs, countless charges of importing illegal firearms and many shipments of drugs. We have detected fingerprints on the envelope you gave to Johannas along with Hec's too, I might add; you were unaware that one packet of drugs was left in the crate that you sent to the Moorabbin factory; were you? There is also a witness to the fact that you had prior knowledge of the plot to kill Larry. Ray witnessed that. There is also the charge of attempted murder of one of our agents, Ray Cress!"

"Agent?"

Drew's face went purple as he pushed aside an officer and, two handed because of the handcuffs, grabbed a pistol out of the holster of the officer and tried to kill Ray.

Drew Slimmery was shot dead in a hail of fire in protection of an unarmed man.

The End

22/9/2001.